"I have a gun," Sparrow said

He kicked the air marshal, who was sitting on the floor, his face a mess of burns and blood. The man groaned. "And I have a hostage."

"No, what you have is a problem," Bolan said, edging closer. "You're only going to get one shot, and I'm fairly certain you're not good enough to hit me, even this close. And if you miss, one of four things will happen." Bolan slid forward another few inches. "One, you'll punch a hole in the plane itself. Not a big deal, really, despite what movies would have you believe."

Sparrow was staring at him with wary fascination, like a rat watching an approaching snake.

"Two, you'll pop a window, which is worse. Someone could get sucked out and the cabin will be filled with so much flying debris that a concussion will be the least of your worries. Three, your bullet clips some wiring. You might stop the in-flight entertainment or you could kill the radar or something worse. And four, your errant shot could puncture one of the fuel tanks. Which, if we're lucky, just causes a fire, but if we're not…" Bolan spread his hands. "Boom."

MACK BOLAN ®

The Executioner

THE EXECUTIONER

DON PENDLETON'S

ARCTIC KILL

A GOLD EAGLE BOOK FROM

WORLDWIDE®

TORONTO • NEW YORK • LONDON
AMSTERDAM • PARIS • SYDNEY • HAMBURG
STOCKHOLM • ATHENS • TOKYO • MILAN
MADRID • WARSAW • BUDAPEST • AUCKLAND

Recycling programs
for this product may
not exist in your area.

First edition August 2014

ISBN-13: 978-0-373-64429-2

Special thanks and acknowledgment to
Joshua Reynolds for his contribution to this work.

ARCTIC KILL

Printed in U.S.A.

There is nothing more inglorious than that glory that is gained by war.
—Thomas More, *Utopia*

I don't fight for glory, power or wealth. My War Everlasting has only one goal: justice...by any means necessary.
—Mack Bolan

THE
MACK BOLAN
LEGEND

Nothing less than a war could have fashioned the destiny of the man called Mack Bolan. Bolan earned the Executioner title in the jungle hell of Vietnam.

But this soldier also wore another name—Sergeant Mercy. He was so tagged because of the compassion he showed to wounded comrades-in-arms and Vietnamese civilians.

Mack Bolan's second tour of duty ended prematurely when he was given emergency leave to return home and bury his family, victims of the Mob. Then he declared a one-man war against the Mafia.

He confronted the Families head-on from coast to coast, and soon a hope of victory began to appear. But Bolan had broken society's every rule. That same society started gunning for this elusive warrior—to no avail.

So Bolan was offered amnesty to work within the system against terrorism. This time, as an employee of Uncle Sam, Bolan became Colonel John Phoenix. With a command center at Stony Man Farm in Virginia, he and his new allies—Able Team and Phoenix Force—waged relentless war on a new adversary: the KGB.

But when his one true love, April Rose, died at the hands of the Soviet terror machine, Bolan severed all ties with Establishment authority.

Now, after a lengthy lone-wolf struggle and much soul-searching, the Executioner has agreed to enter an "arm's-length" alliance with his government once more, reserving the right to pursue personal missions in his Everlasting War.

Reno, Nevada

The heat of a Nevada summer sun beat down on the forecourt of the Rancho Santo Motel with hammerlike intensity. The parking lot was practically sizzling, even in the few scraps of available shade, but Mack Bolan, aka the Executioner, felt the cool patience of a hunter.

Idly, he reached up to scratch at the stubble that coated his jaw. Three days ago, Bolan had agreed to take on a mission for Hal Brognola, and the soldier hadn't shaved since. He was squatting between the motel trash bins, a mostly empty bottle of cheap liquor clutched in his grimy fingers, and his threadbare thrift store duds reeking of booze, sweat and an all-prevalent odor of urine. He'd gotten used to the smell by the second day. "Small favors," he murmured. It was a good disguise. No one saw street people, not if they could help it.

He shifted his weight. The sound-suppressed Beretta 93R holstered at the small of his back was a comforting presence. More easily concealable than his normal sidearm, the Beretta could be set to fire a

3-round burst. It had a 20-round magazine, plus one in the chamber. Bolan swept the Rancho Santo with his keen gaze, scanning the peeling paint, the rust on the piping and the filthy windows. All in all, it was a depressing place. Perhaps that was the point. Who would look for one of the past century's leading research scientists in a place like this?

Bolan had seen the man called E. E. Ackroyd only once since he'd begun his stakeout. Ackroyd was in his late sixties, if Bolan was any judge, but still fairly spry. He dressed like a stereotypical retiree and seemed to spend his days smoking, drinking and reading. At one time, he'd been one of the country's leading microbiologists and could have easily won a Nobel Prize if his research hadn't been part of some hush-hush, black-bag Cold War shenanigans. Or so Brognola had intimated.

Regardless, if his current residence was any indication, Ackroyd seemed to have fallen on hard times, and they were only going to get harder. Someone had set their sights on Ackroyd and targeted him for a snatch and grab. Sadly, who was behind it and why it was planned hadn't been as easy to determine.

The big Fed had sounded worried on the phone. That wasn't unusual; while Hal Brognola was one of the most unflappable men Bolan had ever met, he was also a man burdened by a weight of responsibility that would have crushed Atlas. Bolan wouldn't trade places with his old ally for anything in the world. Brognola fought on fields far removed from Bolan's experience, waging quiet wars in the back rooms of the Wonderland on the Potomac, his only weapons words and favors and influence.

Beneath his mask of grime and stubble, the Executioner smiled thinly. Brognola had been one of his most tenacious opponents once upon a time, in charge of the task force assigned to bring the Executioner to heel. Now they were brothers-in-arms. War makes for strange bedfellows, Bolan mused, especially a war like ours. His smile faded.

Brognola had been worried, but not for the usual reasons. There was something stirring, according to certain back-channel sources. There were ripples spreading in the ocean of information that the world's intelligence agencies trawled, but they weren't being caused by the usual suspects. Brognola wasn't a man to sit on such a warning, and neither was Bolan. The information was too ephemeral for any organization or group to act on—even Brognola's Sensitive Operations Group—but the Executioner could do as he damn well pleased. Bolan had haunted the motel like a ragged ghost for three days. He knew that Ackroyd paid by the week and had been there for a number of years. If Ackroyd was hiding from someone, he'd been doing it for a while. Most of the rooms in the motel were empty, and those that weren't were occupied by nervous transients, drunken tourists, illegal immigrants, meth addicts and a transsexual prostitute named Sheena. Gunshots weren't exactly background noise in this part of Reno but the police weren't likely to be called with any alacrity, which meant he could do what he needed to do without fear of being interrupted. Bolan hoped for Brognola's sake that it wouldn't be too messy.

That hope died when a black SUV pulled into the parking lot. The men who got out were hard cases.

Bolan could tell by the way they moved and the set of
their faces and the telltale bulges beneath their off-the-
rack sport coats. White, middle-aged, trained muscle,
rather than the gym-rat variety. They wore muted col-
ors and dressed business casual. They could have been
salesmen or FBI agents or hit men. Everything about
them spoke of innocuous care—a chameleon-like desire to blend in to the pastel and stucco of the motel.
They were nobody and no one, and that alone would
have pricked Bolan's curiosity. He knew, with a certainty born of grim experience, that he was going to
have to kill at least one of them.

Their voices lost to the wheezing roar of a dozen air
conditioners, the three men climbed the outside stairs
of the motel. They moved with purpose, but without
hurry. Why rush, when their prey didn't know they
were coming?

Bolan had asked Brognola why Ackroyd hadn't
been taken into protective custody at Stony Man,
given that they knew someone wanted him. The answer had been callous in its simplicity. They needed
to know *who* wanted Ackroyd as much as why. More-
over, Brognola wanted to know why Ackroyd, who
knew what he knew, whatever it was, was allowed to
live out his days in a flea-trap motel in Reno. So the
old man was bait, and Bolan the hunter.

"Try to keep one of them breathing," Brognola had
said. Bolan had made no promises, but he knew the
value of information. They were boxing shadows,
and getting some light—any light—would be helpful. Bolan wasn't a fan of situations like these—too
much could go wrong. There was too much they didn't

know. But when the situation warranted it, Bolan had little problem dealing himself in.

Bolan stood, still clutching the bottle. He'd poured most of it over his clothes, but there was still enough remaining to slosh softly. Wobbling slightly, the Executioner stumbled in the direction of the stairs, his eyes on the trio as they ascended. They hadn't noticed him yet.

Bolan stumbled up the stairs, moving with deceptive speed. They had stopped in front of a room on the third floor. Two men stood to either side of the door and the third knocked politely. When Ackroyd didn't answer he knocked again, a bit more forcefully. By the time Bolan had reached the third level, the knocker had stepped back and was readying himself to give the door a kick. He paused when one of the men gestured to the Executioner.

Bolan took his cue and broke into song. He swung the bottle back and forth for emphasis and weaved toward them. The closest man intercepted him. "Be off with you," he said tersely. His accent was harsh and Teutonic-sounding. *German, possibly,* Bolan mused. "Pitch him down the damn stairs," the knocker barked. He was American, probably Nebraskan, Bolan thought. The German reached for him, apparently intent on following the orders.

Bolan staggered back, forcing the German to pursue him. When the man reached for him, Bolan flipped the bottle around with a quick twist of his wrist, grabbed it by its neck and brought it up and across the German's skull. Contrary to every bar brawl seen on film, a good bottle rarely broke when you hit someone with it. But it did the job well enough.

The German toppled onto the Executioner, who caught him, shoved him aside and snatched the Beretta from his holster even as the German fell. Bolan fired. The member of the trio who hadn't yet spoken pitched backward with a yell. The Nebraskan, caught flat-footed, clawed for his own weapon. "No," Bolan said. A minute and a half had elapsed.

The Nebraskan's hand froze. "Back away from the door," Bolan said and jerked his chin for emphasis. He stepped over the unconscious German and drew close to the door. The man backed away, hands spread.

"Police?" the Nebraskan asked.

"Not quite," Bolan said.

"We've got money," the Nebraskan said, licking his lips.

"Small world, so do I," Bolan replied. "I want information."

The Nebraskan's eyes went flat. He said nothing. Bolan gestured with the Beretta. "Downstairs. We're going for a ride."

"No," the Nebraskan said harshly.

Bolan hesitated. He was a good judge of character. Some men could be pushed and threatened. Bolan himself was not one of them, but from the tone of the Nebraskan's voice, it seemed he wasn't, either. Or at least, he hadn't reached the point where he could be… yet. That was a problem. They needed information, but the man before him wasn't likely to provide it. And Bolan couldn't leave him or let him go, not without knowing what was going on. The door opened. Ackroyd's eyes widened as he took in the scene. His mouth was half-open, a cigarette dangling from his bottom lip. The Nebraskan threw himself at the old man. Before Bolan could take him out, a pistol snarled, biting into the wall of the motel. Plaster and Sheetrock spattered his cheek.

The man Bolan had shot moments earlier had pulled his piece. The front of his shirt was red and his eyes were unfocused, but even a dying man could be dangerous. He fired again and Bolan lunged to the side, his hip connecting painfully with the rail of the walkway. The Beretta spoke eloquently and the wounded man fell back, his weapon clattering to the ground.

Bolan turned. The Nebraskan stepped out of the room, holding Ackroyd in front of him. He had his weapon pressed against the old man's head. The Nebraskan said nothing. He didn't even glance at the dead man. He simply backed away, dragging Ackroyd with him. Bolan began to follow, the Beretta extended. "Stop," the Nebraskan said, "or I'll paint the wall with his brain."

"I don't think so," Bolan said, without stopping. "I think you need him and his brain intact. That sound about right, Mr. Ackroyd?"

Ackroyd cleared his throat. He looked frightened, but he was controlling himself. Bolan's estimation of Ackroyd climbed a few notches. "I—and I want to be clear about this—have no idea what's going on," the old man said, his voice rusty from years of drink and cigarettes.

"Quiet," the Nebraskan said.

"You're being kidnapped, Mr. Ackroyd. Do you have any idea why that might be happening?" Bolan asked calmly. Sweat stung his eyes, but he didn't blink. He concentrated on the Nebraskan.

"Who's asking?" Ackroyd said. The old man had guts. Bolan was impressed.

"The man who's trying to keep you alive," Bolan replied. The Nebraskan took another step back. Bolan took another step forward.

"I was told this place was safe," Ackroyd said. "I was told I'd be left alone."

"Somebody lied," Bolan said, "or made a mistake."

"Probably both," Ackroyd agreed.

"Shut up," the Nebraskan snapped. His grip on Ackroyd tightened. The old man winced as the Nebraskan's arm flexed against his throat. He had pluck, but he was still on the wrong side of sixty, and hadn't been keeping himself in shape.

"I can keep this up all day, friend," Bolan said, a note of menace creeping into his voice. "Let him go."

Something in the Nebraskan's eyes made Bolan tense. A shadow crossed the ground in front of him. Big arms snapped tight around him like the jaws of a trap and he was jerked from his feet even as the air was squeezed out of his lungs. Bolan gasped. The German had recovered, and far more quickly than Bolan had anticipated. The Nebraskan had been drawing him out, giving his compatriot time to recover.

The German shook him, and Bolan lost his grip on the Beretta. "Go, Sparrow!" the German shouted as he squeezed Bolan hard enough to make his ribs creak. "Take the old man and go. I will handle this fool! *Vril-YA!*"

Bolan grunted and drove his head back, into the German's face. He heard bone crunch and the grip on him loosened. Bolan slithered free and dropped to the ground. He twisted around and drove a hard blow into the German's belly. The man gasped and staggered, but didn't fall. His fists smashed down on Bolan's head and shoulders like hammers. The Executioner lunged forward, tackling his opponent. They crashed against the wall.

The German was strong and he knew how to fight. But Bolan knew how to win. Two swift, savage strikes to the German's kidneys made him gasp in agony. He responded with a knee to Bolan's groin. The Executioner caught the blow and sank his fingers into the meat of the man's knee, twisting savagely as he rammed his palm into a momentarily vulnerable windpipe. The German fell back against the wall, gagging. Bolan didn't let him recover. He unleashed a rapid salvo of precise hammerblows to the man's belly and sides.

The German stayed on his feet with a tenacity that was almost impressive. Wheezing, he lunged. His fingers clawed at Bolan's face and throat, and the Executioner found himself forced back until his spine connected with the rail. Bolan shoved his arms up and swatted aside the German's hands. The heel of Bolan's palm struck his opponent's already mangled nose, forcing fragments of splintered cartilage and bone up toward the man's brain. Bolan spun as the German pitched backward with a gurgle.

The Nebraskan—Sparrow—hadn't wasted any time. He'd dragged Ackroyd down the stairwell on the other side of the walkway and shoved the old man into the SUV. He was climbing in himself when he saw Bolan looking down at him. Sparrow cursed and raised his weapon. He fired, driving Bolan back from the rail. The SUV's engine growled to life and gravel crunched beneath its tires. Bolan sprang to his feet, caught the rail and swung his legs over. He dropped onto the SUV as it backed out of its parking spot, the force of impact radiating upward through the soles of his boots to his skull. Unprepared, he was flung off his feet as Sparrow twisted the wheel, whipping the vehicle around. Bolan rolled off the roof and slid down the windshield, striking the hood. He scrambled desperately to keep from slipping off and falling beneath the vehicle's wheels.

Then, in a squeal of rubber, the SUV cut a sharp turn and hurtled out of the parking lot, taking the Executioner with it.

2

Anchorage, Alaska

Saul Mervin stubbed out his cigarette. On the television, the President was addressing Congress. Mervin looked at the digital timer on the television set that occupied one wall of his hotel room. Nevada was an hour ahead of Alaska, he recalled. That meant Sparrow's call was only an hour late. He lay back on the bed and closed his eyes, not to sleep, but to think. There could be many reasons for the delay.

Mervin was a spare man, lacking any excess flesh or muscle. He was a thing of narrow specifications, with a chin like a scoop and eyes the color of faded dollar bills. He lacked distinguishing features, the work of years and a careful attention to detail. No agency had his fingerprints or photos on file, and his DNA was sacrosanct.

Without opening his eyes, Mervin reached over and plucked a cigarette from the silver case on the nightstand, popped it between his thin lips and lit it with a cheap lighter. As soon as he'd arrived he'd pulled the smoke detector off the wall and opened a window. He needed nicotine more than warmth. The feeling of smoke slithering through his lungs helped him organize his thoughts.

If Sparrow were any other man, Mervin would suspect a distraction—a woman or an accident. But Sparrow was Sparrow. He was single-minded and utterly devoted to the Society. The others with him were equally dedicated, if not so single-minded. That left the possibility of interference. Mervin frowned. He had factored in sixteen possible points of interference for the Reno operation. Seventeen, if he counted betrayal. Immediately, he discarded the thought. Sparrow was Sparrow. He would continue with the mission regardless. The man was determined, if nothing else.

He mentally flicked through the remaining sixteen, weighing the variables and considering the likelihood of each. Interpol wasn't likely—he had organized the Viennese operation specifically to distract them. The FBI was a leaky sieve; Mervin would have gotten word of their interference through the usual channels. On and on he went, rapidly considering, weighing and discarding the possibilities.

He had always possessed the ability to process and analyze with computer-like efficiency. Even as a child, numbers and calculations had proven no mystery to him. He saw the patterns that no one else could see. He saw the bigger picture. It was the only picture that mattered—his picture.

But now his plans were threatened. His cheek twitched and he inhaled carcinogens. Like a spider whose web was damaged, he could repair it, but only by acting quickly.

Someone knocked on the door. "It's open, Kraft," he called out. Only one person would bother to knock.

The door opened to admit a heavy, long-limbed shape. Rolf Kraft was a big, dangerous-looking man, as befitted a former member of the *Kommando Spezialkrafte*. Kraft had been one of the best the German Special Forces had to offer. Now he was Mervin's nursemaid.

Kraft's nose wrinkled as he caught sight of the cigarette. With a grunt, he plucked it from between Mervin's lips and stubbed it out. "You shouldn't smoke. It's bad for you," he said. Kraft had barely the trace of an accent, making it easy for him to blend in in most Western countries. He spoke fluent English, French, German and Russian. And like Sparrow, he was utterly and completely dedicated to the aims and goals of the Society of Thylea.

Kraft had killed on behalf of the Society for a number of years. Academics, historians, explorers and government agents had died by his hands, or the hands of those he'd trained. He could pluck a fly from flight with a rifle, or plant an explosive device so cunningly that its presence would be overlooked, even in the aftermath. He also had little compunction about engaging in more close-up work; indeed, he preferred it. That preference had seen him drummed out of the Special Forces and into the waiting arms of the Society.

"Smoking helps me think," Mervin said. His tone skirted petulance, and a flash of annoyance rippled across the surface of his amazing brain. Kraft could get under his skin simply by choosing the wrong moment to exhale.

"You think too much. Also bad for you," Kraft said. Another flash of annoyance; Mervin looked at Kraft and calmed himself by calculating the six points of weakness by which Kraft could be disabled from their current relative positions.

"Probably, but that is why I am in charge," Mervin said, sitting up. That was true, as far as it went. But he had no true authority. Kraft was the muscle, and if the muscle failed, not even the most efficient brain could make it work. He picked up another cigarette, caught sight of Kraft's face and stuck it behind his ear. "Sparrow hasn't called."

Kraft's face betrayed nothing, but his eyes slid to the satellite phone on the desk in the corner. "Interference," he said. He knew the routine as well as Mervin did. Better, most likely, though he would never say so. Kraft's loyalty was like iron. He appeared to regard Mervin as a sibling, someone to be protected or coddled. Whether that was due to the orders of their immediate superiors—who, Mervin knew, valued him—or because of some snag in Kraft's emotional makeup, Mervin did not know, nor did he care.

"Possibly," Mervin said. "We will act as if that is the case." He pulled an old-fashioned pocket watch out of his coat pocket and opened it. It was his only memento, a gift from his mother. Or so he assumed. He had not known her well and barely recalled her voice. "We will give them an additional hour. If they haven't called by then, we continue with the plan." That, too, was part of the routine, a routine Mervin had spent years crafting. The servants of the Society of Thylea operated like well-oiled clockwork. If one gear slipped or was stripped, another took its place. Mervin appreciated clockwork. Besides nicotine, only the click of clockwork could soothe his mind when it skipped its track. The regular rhythm settled his heart rate and helped him slide his thoughts into their proper alignment.

"Without Ackroyd, it's going to be difficult," Kraft said. He scraped his palm across his freshly shaved chin, thinking. Mervin hated the sound flesh on stubble made. It grated on his nerves. He snapped the watch closed.

"But not impossible."

"No," Kraft agreed. He smiled. "Nothing is impossible for us. It will be a great day, the day after it is done. It will be a new era for the pure peoples, *Vril-YA!*"

"Yes, yes, *Vril-YA,*" Mervin agreed. He wished, sometimes, that he had Kraft's devotion to the Promise of Tomorrow. But the ruthless, implacable logic that made Mervin useful to the Society also prevented him from fully buying into the Nazi bedtime story that had propelled them for almost a century.

Facts shifted in the Rolodex of his mind. Where Kraft was an engine of destruction, Mervin was an engine of calculation, and as such, he collected facts and fancies with a glutton's instinctive frenzy. The Society had first flown the banners of Thylea in 1918, envisioning a hyperborean mega-continent of ice-sculpture citadels and pure-blooded Nordic giants linked to the *Vril,* the life-blood of the cosmos. A *Jotunheim* Utopia, where gods and giants were one and the same, that ruled over the past and future of the Aryan Race. The Society of Thylea had been founded on the principles of that nonexistent continent, and was ruthless in seeking to bring about their particular melanin-based *Ragnarok.* They longed to create the Aryan utopia only dreamt of by frantic xenophobes, believing that it would bring a sacred peace to the world.

It was all rot, of course. In Mervin's opinion, there was no more truth to these tales than to the stories of the Bible or the Koran. Stories told to justify and rationalize a campaign of murder and obfuscation that had been going on for almost a hundred years. Men like Kraft clung to the stories of Thylea with brutal naiveté. But Mervin was a man of logic. He saw little need to waste energy on self-justification. Not when there were more important matters at hand.

In the aftermath of World War II, the Society of Thylea had gone underground, as had so many groups and persons with ties to the Nazis. Unlike those groups, however, the Society had money, and lots of it. Even today it had its financial supporters. And using the resources of those supporters, the Society had, for decades, hunted for weapons it could employ in its battle against the lesser races. It had sought to find the singular spear of destiny it could thrust into the heart of sub-humanity.

And, eventually, it had found something, in a place called HYPERBOREA.

It was pure poetry, that name. And a fair amount of serendipity, too.

Mervin was growing tired of the Society. More, he was growing tired of Kraft. He looked at the big man, his expression bland, imagining Kraft broken, bloody and dead. There was no particular reason for his enmity. It was simply his nature. Familiarity bred contempt. He was good at hiding it, he thought. If any of them suspected, they said nothing.

"Are the others ready?" he asked.

Kraft frowned. "If not, I'll have their hides."

"That wasn't what I asked."

Kraft grinned. "So precise," he said. "Yes, they are ready. The charter plane has been booked. We will deal with the pilot on the day, given that we don't need her." He made a face. "She is a native. Likely a bad pilot, anyway."

"Given the reviews of her business, I doubt that," Mervin said. He sighed as he caught Kraft's deepening frown. "A bad pilot is statistically unlikely to care for his plane, or to have a reputation that guarantees noninterference. Neither of those things would be of help to us. I chose the best pilot available. Ergo, she is a good pilot."

"I meant no insult," Kraft said, smiling slightly. He patted Mervin's shoulder. "And what if Sparrow calls?"

"Then we follow through with the current plan. We will meet the others at the airport and escort Dr. Ackroyd to the charter plane. You will dispose of the pilot in front of Ackroyd, as an object lesson, and then we will go to meet our destiny."

"Object lesson, eh?"

"Waste not, want not," Mervin said. Kraft laughed heartily. Mervin hated that laugh.

The Society thought HYPERBOREA would mean a new beginning.

And for Saul Mervin, it would.

3

Reno, Nevada

Bolan's fingers scrabbled at the hood of the SUV as he fought to hold on. The vibration of the engine thrummed through him and he felt as if his teeth might rattle loose from his jaw. Horns blared as the vehicle bulled through traffic, weaving back and forth across the median as it roared toward Reno's commercial district. Bolan hooked his feet into the front grille and tried to shove himself up, but the SUV was simply moving too fast and his own weight was acting against him. He grabbed for the hood ornament and it snapped away in his hand. His arms and legs ached with tension and he knew it was only a matter of time until he lost his grip or was dislodged from his perch by a speed bump.

Traffic whipped around the Executioner in a blur of lights and sounds. The SUV jerked to the side and, caught by surprise, Bolan half swung off the front end, cursing, before he crashed back against the vehicle and regained his grip. He had to get off the SUV and soon. He could make out the thin squeal of distant sirens. The police weren't far behind. The way Sparrow was driving, he wouldn't be able to avoid their notice. Maybe he didn't intend to. Bolan met Sparrow's furious gaze through the cracked windshield. The kidnapper wasn't happy about his stowaway. Bolan wasn't exactly enthused himself. If he'd been thinking more clearly, he'd have let Sparrow go and simply followed. But there hadn't been time to think. He'd been determined to bring down the last of the kidnappers, and now he was clinging to the front of an erratically driven SUV. If Bolan had his KA-BAR combat knife, he might've been able to punch a hole in the radiator, but as it was, he was at the mercy of gravity and physics and unless he acted—and soon—he was going to suffer the same fate as every unlucky insect ever to strike a windshield.

The SUV began to weave again. A four-door sedan was brushed aside in a scream of crumpled metal and shattered glass. Bolan hunched forward. The SUV drifted to the side and Bolan realized that Sparrow was trying to scrape him off. Twisting his head, he saw that they were approaching the Virginia Street Bridge. That would have to be his stop. Bolan felt a twinge of regret at having to leave Ackroyd in the hands of his captor, but there was nothing for it. He wouldn't do Ackroyd much good smeared across downtown Reno. *I won't do anyone much good that way,* he thought grimly. Too much was depending on him.

With a grunt of effort, Bolan began to make his way down the grille. Grit thrown up by the wheels stung his eyes and face. His shoulders and hips burned. Moving carefully, the Executioner lowered himself between the front wheels of the SUV. He was only going to get one shot at getting off this ride. Luckily, he'd been in similar situations before. He wedged his lean frame between the wheels and hooked his feet around the rear axle. Clutching the bottom of the SUV's frame, Bolan began working himself toward the back of the speeding vehicle, his body mere inches from the street. Exhaust filled his mouth and lungs. His muscles were screaming by the time he reached the back end of the vehicle.

The SUV bumped as it drove onto the bridge. Bolan nearly lost his grip and he felt something in his shoulder pop. His legs struck the street and for a moment he was being dragged behind the SUV on his back. The road seemed to rise up to meet him like a hungry predator, and the hard, hot surface kissed his back. His shirt and pullover were shredded and his body armor seemed to provide no protection at all. With a hiss of pain, he flipped himself around. The throbbing in his shoulder grew and was joined by a dull ache between his shoulder blades. His eyes found the license tag and, acting on impulse, he reached out and hooked it with his fingers. He tore it free with a single, sharp jerk and then, after checking behind him for oncoming traffic, let go.

Bolan curled into a ball as he rolled across the bridge, tucking in his arms and legs. He struck the rail, hard, and all of the air whooshed out of his lungs as he uncoiled. He still held the SUV's tag. Bolan grabbed the side of the bridge and hauled himself to his feet. Pain sparks burst and spun across his eyes and he felt like a water-balloon punctured by a stick. The bridge was two lanes wide, coming and going. The Truckee River was a placid, dark mirror running beneath it. Bolan spat blood. His lip was mashed and torn, and his body was bruised up one side and down the other. He'd made it off in one piece, but just barely. Out of the corner of his eye, he saw a flash of blue lights. He needed to move, and fast.

Ignoring his protesting muscles, and clutching the license tag, the Executioner grabbed the wrought iron railing that lined the bridge and jumped over it. He hit the water feet first, crossing his arms over his chest. The water wasn't deep, but it was enough to cushion his landing. As he surfaced, he saw a low, ornate rock wall that lined the opposite bank. Above, on the bridge, horns honked and sirens wailed. The police were in pursuit, but it was too much to hope that they'd catch Sparrow. Spitting water, he headed for the rock wall.

It took him an hour to get back to his designated Reno safe house; it was a rare taxi that wanted to pick up a bedraggled, sopping-wet bum, much less one that was bleeding. When he'd finally caught one, it was already late afternoon.

The safe house—located in the Chisholm Trailer Park—was one of several Bolan had scattered over the state of Nevada. During his war against the Mafia, Bolan had been to Nevada more than once, hunting his prey through the neon jungles of Las Vegas and Reno. Bolan didn't use this safe house much these days. It was registered under the name of Frank LaMancha, an old alias he used when posing as a Black Ace.

The mobile home was a Spartan affair—a rumpled bed, an unplugged fridge and, of course, the armory. After closing the door and pulling the blinds, he carefully moved the bed aside, folded up the carpet and opened the hidden hatch built into the floor. Inside was his gear from an earlier operation. Fatigues, a second set of body armor, web gear, the UMP and spare ammunition, his combat knife and a backup pistol. He extracted the Desert Eagle and checked the magazine. He wasn't happy about losing the Beretta, but the motel was likely already a crime scene. It would end up in an evidence locker somewhere, unclaimed and forgotten. He could get another easily enough, but like all craftsmen, Bolan hated to lose a proven tool.

In truth, however, he preferred the Desert Eagle. For sheer stopping power, that particular gas-operated, semi-automatic pistol was hard to beat. It could quickly be converted to fire a wide range of ammunition, from .44 to .357 Magnum calibers.

He put the pistol aside and set about peeling off his stinking clothes. He grimaced as he took off the light armored vest he'd been wearing beneath his thrift store secondhands. The material had been scraped from the metal and the vest looked like it had lost a fight with a bobcat. He tossed it into the hatch and went to take a shower. Bolan spent longer under the thin spray of lukewarm water than he'd intended. The water stung the abrasions that marked his body, making him wince. But the pain helped him to organize his thoughts. The Executioner's ability to observe and recall, even without consciously intending to do so, was second to none.

The kidnappers' weapons had been store bought. That meant they weren't working for the government, under contract or otherwise. Professionals picked up weapons wherever their target was, usually from a previously established contact. The clothes had been newly purchased, as well. They were off-the-rack—from a department store.

Everything about the men he'd fought screamed disposable—their clothes, weapons and transportation; all of it was cheap and easy to replace. Even their lives. The German had willingly sacrificed himself so that the Nebraskan—Sparrow—could escape with Ackroyd. That spoke to either personal loyalty or fanaticism. What had the German yelled as he'd attacked? *Vril-YA*… What did that mean? The phrase was somehow familiar.

He stepped out of the shower, dried off and wrapped the towel around his waist. Then, sitting on the edge of his bed, he used his satellite phone to make contact with Stony Man Farm.

Brognola answered after the first ring. Bolan smiled slightly, imagining the big Fed fretting near the phone. "Striker—what the hell happened?" Brognola asked. "It's all over the local news—the shoot-out, the SUV, all of it."

"I got careless," Bolan said and his smile faded. That wasn't strictly true, but he saw little reason to sugarcoat the failure.

Brognola snorted. "Bull. They just got lucky. It happens to the best of us, once in a while. What about Ackroyd?"

"They got him. Well—he got him. There was only one kidnapper left. We went for a bit of a drive and then I went for a quick swim. I don't think they're planning to kill him, though. Not after what they went through to get him," Bolan said. He bent and picked up the license tag. "I have something that might be of use." He rattled off the plate number. "I got it off

the SUV they were using. It's probably a rental, or
stolen, but I'm betting on the former. I'm also betting
that address is wherever they're forting up. If you can
find an address…"

"I can do better than that," Brognola said. "I can
pinpoint where they are and send backup. Lyons and
Able Team—"

"No time for that," Bolan said. "Just get me that
address. I'll handle it from there."

"Striker—"

"Address," Bolan said, cutting him short. "You
dealt me in, don't complain about how I play my hand.
If I need help, I'll call. You know that."

"I know, Striker." Brognola sounded tired. "Address in ten."

"While we're waiting, let me talk to Aaron," Bolan
said. Aaron Kurtzman was Stony Man's burly com-
puter expert. Brognola did as Bolan requested.

"Striker, you're missing one excellent pot of coffee
today," Kurtzman said, and the phone vibrated with
the sound of his subsequent slurp. Bolan winced at the
thought of Kurtzman's particular concept of coffee.
Swill was a more accurate term, in Bolan's opinion.
It was a gut check to even get past the first mouthful.

"Sounds heavenly," Bolan said. "Have you ever
heard the phrase *Vril-YA* before?"

"*Vril-YA,* huh," Kurtzman said, sounding amused.
"Bulwer-Lytton replaced Cervantes as your favorite
wordslinger?"

"Bulwer-Lytton," Bolan said. Suddenly, it clicked.
"Edward Bulwer-Lytton. I knew I'd heard that somewhere before." An English author, Bulwer-Lytton had
written a novel called *The Coming Race,* in 1871. The

book was about a subterranean master race and their deadly energy weapon and had been one of the most badly written pieces of tripe Bolan had ever laid eyes on. "I need you to cross-reference that book with any sort of organization. Specifically ones that might want to kidnap a man like E. E. Ackroyd."

"Seriously?" Kurtzman asked, his tone edged with disbelief.

"Have you ever known me not to be serious?" Bolan asked.

Brognola came back on the line. It had taken him less than ten minutes to roust his contacts for the address tied to the license plate. As Bolan had suspected, it was a rental. "We're back-tracing the credit card that was used to rent it," Brognola said. "It's probably a fraudulent account, but we'll put a trace on it, just in case they use it again." He gave Bolan the address and added, "Are you sure you don't want to wait for backup? According to the Reno PD, your playmate used that SUV to bull through a barricade. He nearly ran down several officers and ditched it in a parking garage."

"Someone picked him up," Bolan said. It wasn't a question.

"Which means it wasn't just those three," Brognola said. "You're looking at multiple hostiles who've already shown they don't particularly care about starting a public ruckus."

"Then the sooner they're taken off the board, the better," Bolan said firmly.

Brognola sighed. "Be careful, Striker."

"Always am," Bolan said and hung up.

Satisfied, he tossed the phone onto the bed. Then, without hurry, he began to dress for the battle to come.

4

Sparrow stared at the phone as if it were a snake preparing to strike. He gnawed his bottom lip. Mervin wasn't going to like hearing that his meticulously crafted plans had fallen through. At least Kraft was safely in Anchorage with the psychotic little android and not anywhere close enough to wring Sparrow's neck.

To say that things had not gone well was an understatement. No one should have known about Ackroyd, save themselves. But someone had been there, and that someone had made quite an impression. Indeed, thanks to the nameless antagonist's interference, Sparrow had almost been caught by the Reno police before he'd managed to abandon the SUV and meet with the others. He hoped that their unknown attacker—Ackroyd had sworn he didn't recognize the man—was now just a greasy spot on the street.

Luckily, the license tag for the SUV had vanished during the chase. That meant they had some time before the police tracked the vehicle to the rental agency and then traced the credit card they'd used. The card would lead the authorities back here—to the SunCo warehouse they were using as a base—and to the company itself, one of a dozen Society fronts in the greater United States.

Mervin had assured Sparrow that even if the authorities discovered the credit card and the identities attached to it, they could always burn the warehouse. To Mervin's way of thinking, most things could be solved by the proper application of bullets and/or gasoline. He was a straight-ahead thinker, Mervin.

It was all about speed with him, a speed and precision that escaped most of the soldiers the Society employed. Mervin was inhuman, and so was Kraft, come to think of it, but those who followed Mervin's orders were only too mortal, Sparrow reflected sourly, and he included himself in that estimation.

Sparrow had joined the Society of Thylea as a young man. His father had been a member, and his father's father. It was a tradition, and a good one, since the Society offered more than any church or political movement. It wasn't just talk. The Society was determined to bring back the age of titans, free of the shackles imposed by lesser, weaker races.

Sparrow deeply, desperately wanted to be a hero. And he would be, if they succeeded. He and the others would be the heroes of a new age, venerated and immortalized in song and film. He comforted himself with the thought of what was to come.

"It's not going to get better, the longer you hesitate," Alexi said, leaning against the office door. "Just call him."

Sparrow looked at Alexi and frowned. The big Russian was a bottle blond, with a face like a mattock and shoulders like a stretched coat hanger. There was more Eurasian in him than the Society normally liked, but between the hair dye and his ability to recite the *Volsunga Saga,* people made allowances. He'd been a member of some Moscow-based Neo-Nazi group before he'd joined the Society, and the tattoos that covered his arms told a story as brutal as any old Aryan saga.

Behind Alexi, out in the warehouse proper, Sparrow could see the others. They were packing up their gear and preparing for the exodus to come. Counting Alexi and himself, there were only eight men. There had been ten, but their mysterious attacker had seen to Horst and Bridges. Sparrow felt a flicker of guilt for abandoning Horst. The big German had been right, of course. The mission was the only important thing. Their lives meant nothing next to the resurrection of Thylea. Still, it nagged at him. He'd left a fellow paladin—a fellow servant of the holy cause—to die by an assassin's hand. No man blamed him, but Sparrow still felt slightly sick thinking of it.

"Maybe you should call him," Sparrow said acidly.

Alexi made shooing motions with his big, scarred hands. "Oh, no, you are in charge, my friend. Man in charge calls the Tick-Tock Man. Those are the rules."

"Don't call him that," Sparrow said.

"Why? He isn't here. He wouldn't care even if he was." Alexi shrugged. "He is—ah—'tick tock,' yes? Crazy," he said.

Sparrow couldn't argue. Mervin *was* crazy. Not crazy violent or crazy fanatical, but crazy all the same. At some point, Saul Mervin's clockwork had sprung its track and now he bobbed along like a crippled toy. He wasn't a person anymore, but a machine. An abacus with a two-pack-a-day habit.

Nonetheless, the *Sun-Koh*—ruling body of the Society of Thylea—had entrusted many of their operations to Mervin. It was through Mervin that their will was directed and accomplished. The Tick-Tock Man, as Alexi called him, was the Sword of Thylea, and his word was law. It was through him that the Coming World would be revealed. That was why they had come to Reno, in pursuit of the old man. That was why they had been searching for any word of HYPERBOREA, which Sparrow had been half convinced was just a myth concocted by conspiracy theorists.

But Mervin had believed. And now they had found it—the spear they would thrust into the belly of the fallen world, to spill an ocean of blood from which a new, stronger world would be born.

Nonetheless, Mervin was, as Alexi had so eloquently stated, crazy.

"Yes, Alexi, he's crazy. Hence my hesitation," Sparrow grunted. He expelled a shaky breath. Someone had to make a status report. And unfortunately, that someone was him. "Fine, give me the office."

Alexi nodded and stepped out, closing the door behind him. Sparrow cursed softly and picked up the phone. Mervin answered on the first ring. Sparrow shivered, imagining Mervin's pale eyes staring at the phone, waiting for it to ring. It really was like waiting for a snake to strike. "We got him," he said.

"You're late," Mervin replied. His voice was a hollow chirp, high-pitched and mechanical, but not amusing. It stung Sparrow's ears and pride.

"There was interference."

"Inconsequential," Mervin said.

"Decidedly not," Sparrow answered. "Horst and

Bridges are dead. Someone was watching Ackroyd—a bodyguard, maybe. Or someone's rumbled us."

"Inconceivable," Mervin said. Then, "Describe them."

"Him," Sparrow corrected. "Just one man. He was lethal, fast, effective. Dressed like a bum, but moved like—well, like Kraft."

"Identity?" Mervin asked. That was how he spoke to everyone who wasn't Kraft—terse, wasting no words. With Kraft, he was practically loquacious. Sometimes Sparrow pitied Kraft.

"No clue—he didn't identify himself. He just did his level best to kill us."

Mervin was silent for a long moment. Then, "But you have Ackroyd?"

"I do."

"Satisfactory. I wish to speak to him."

Sparrow let out a slow breath. He put the phone down and called out, "Alexi? Send the old man in."

The door opened and Ackroyd stumbled through, thanks to a none-too-gentle shove from the Russian. Ackroyd cursed and turned, but Sparrow caught him by the scruff of the neck and shoved him toward a chair. "Someone wants to talk to you, Doctor. Give him all due attention, if you value your fingers," he snapped, switching the phone to speaker. Ackroyd was proving to be a less-than-docile victim. In fact, the old man had a mouth like a sailor and was steadily, if slowly, tap-dancing on Sparrow's last nerve.

Ackroyd gave Sparrow a rheumy glare.

"Dr. Ackroyd," Mervin said. Ackroyd's glare transferred to the phone.

"I know who I am. Who the blazes are you?"

"I am no one, Dr. Ackroyd. I am a cog in a machine, even as you are." Mervin rattled off an address. It meant nothing to Sparrow, but Ackroyd's eyes widened. The old man slumped back in his chair, his face suddenly pale. For a moment, Sparrow feared he might be having a heart attack. "Do you recognize that address, Dr. Ackroyd?" Mervin asked.

"Yes," Ackroyd said, closing his eyes. He rubbed his face with his hands.

"What is that address, Dr. Ackroyd?"

"How did you get it?" Ackroyd countered.

"Inconsequential. What is that address, Dr. Ackroyd?"

Ackroyd licked his lips. His Adam's apple bobbed as he convulsively swallowed. "My granddaughter," he said softly.

"Correct. It is the address of your granddaughter and her family, including your great-grandchildren. They do not know who you are. But you, via your remaining governmental contacts, know who they are. You watch them. You protect them by pretending to be dead. Now you will protect them by telling me what I want to know."

"HYPERBOREA," Ackroyd croaked.

"You have anticipated me, yes. HYPERBOREA, Dr. Ackroyd. I require your expertise regarding that installation and what it contains." Sparrow thought Mervin sounded almost cheerful.

"If you know about it, you already know what it is," Ackroyd said. Something in his voice gave Sparrow a slight chill. Ackroyd had the look of a man hanggliding over hell.

"Yes," Mervin said.

"You know it can't be used for anything."

"Incorrect," Mervin said. "Its use is manifold. Especially for the organization we represent. In any event, your opinions are superfluous. All we require from you is your presence. You will help us enter HYPERBOREA, Dr. Ackroyd."

"Why me?" Ackroyd asked.

"You are the only member of the project still breathing," Mervin replied. "The others have passed on through a variety of ailments, accidents and simple age-related entropy. You are the last man standing, Dr. Ackroyd."

"Just my luck," Ackroyd muttered.

"Luck is hokum. Luck is for the weak-minded. You will help us, Dr. Ackroyd. You will play ball, or your family will be butchered in their beds."

"And after I help you?"

"You will die. But your family will live, unaware and unharmed." Mervin's voice was flat.

Ackroyd stared at the phone. In that moment, Sparrow almost felt sorry for him. The old man had probably suspected he was living on borrowed time. In his place, Sparrow certainly would have. But to hear it stated so flatly, so baldly, was like a kick to the gut. Idly, he wondered whether Mervin did it on purpose. Maybe the abacus had a sadistic streak beneath the logic.

"Fine," Ackroyd said.

"Good. You may leave. I wish to talk to Mr. Sparrow now."

Sparrow gestured and Alexi stepped in, hooked the old man's arm and jerked him to his feet. Once Sparrow had watched them go he said, "He's gone."

"You have the tickets?"

Annoyed, Sparrow bit back a retort. "Yes," he said. "What'll I do about Horst and Bridges? Their bodies…"

"They are dead and in no position to complain. Forget them. All that matters is getting Ackroyd to Anchorage on schedule. Can you do that, Mr. Sparrow?"

"Of course," Sparrow said, harsher than he'd intended.

"Good. I would hate to see you meet the same fate as Horst and Bridges."

Sparrow licked his lips, suddenly nervous, and asked, "What—ah—what about the interference?"

"What about him? If he tries again, kill him. If not, then it does not matter. All that matters is getting Ackroyd to Anchorage, Mr. Sparrow. That is all you should be concerned with." There was a click. Sparrow stared at the phone for a moment.

"*Vril-YA,* motherfucker," he grunted.

5

The warehouse sat just outside the central business district of Reno. It was surrounded by several blocks of nothing in particular save more warehouses. Being a Sunday, those warehouses were empty and the surrounding area was quiet. From the Executioner's point of view, that was perfect. No one around meant little in the way of potential collateral damage. He hefted the Heckler & Koch and examined it one last time. Such meticulous attention to his equipment had saved his life on more than one occasion.

The address Brognola had run down was gold. Bolan's opponents were either lazy and overconfident, or they didn't plan on staying long after grabbing Ackroyd. The warehouse was registered to SunCo Industries. Bolan had never heard of it. Nonetheless, as he examined the warehouse from the roof of its closest neighbor, he wondered if the address had been chosen at random, or whether there was a connection between these men and where they'd chosen to fort up. But that was a consideration for another time. Better to concentrate on the matter at hand.

A quick scouting foray had revealed a number of cars parked behind the warehouse. Bolan had efficiently disabled all of the vehicles, removing spark plugs or puncturing tires. After that, it had been a simple matter to break into a nearby warehouse and get up to the roof via the HVAC access hatch. Bolan looked up at the sky. It was getting dark, or as dark as it got in Reno.

The Executioner let the UMP dangle from its sling and hefted his Plumett AL-52. The air-launcher was capable of throwing a grappling hook attached to a rope around one hundred meters. Taking aim, he fired. The Plumett gave a soft pop, and the grappling hook sailed over the gap between the two warehouses. The hooks dug into the opposite roof. Bolan gave the rope an experimental tug and then set the Plumett down on its weighted stand. The line would bear his weight long enough for him to get across the gap.

Bolan gripped the line with his gloved hands and swung off the warehouse roof, quickly interlacing his ankles over the rope. He hung suspended over the gap, his back to the ground, his face pointed at the sky. Then, hand over hand, he pulled himself toward his destination.

When Bolan was halfway across, he heard the squeal of hinges from below. He froze, risking a swift, upside-down glance at the ground. A shape moved out of a side door and stepped into the alley between the two warehouses. Bolan's keen gaze caught a spark of light and he smelled the tang of a newly lit cigarette. He waited for a moment. Then, certain the figure below wasn't looking up, Bolan continued to pull himself across the line. When he reached the edge of the roof, he hauled himself over and dropped to his feet, UMP ready. Satisfied that his arrival hadn't been noticed, Bolan located the access hatch and entered the warehouse.

Lowering himself onto the gantry, he scanned the warehouse below. Bolan was well above the fluorescent lights that illuminated the mostly empty building. He could see a delivery truck at the loading dock and the serpentine coil of a conveyer belt that stretched across the interior of the building from one set of loading docks to the other. A few picnic tables and benches were off to the side, near a pair of soda machines and an office. Several men sat or stood nearby, including Ackroyd, who was steadily adding to a small pyramid of smoked-down and stubbed-out cigarette butts on the concrete floor between his feet. Ackroyd looked frightened. Bolan couldn't blame him.

The men were a hard-looking lot. All white, all dressed like tourists… But tourists didn't carry AR-15s and what appeared to be SIG-Pro semi-automatic pistols. There were six of them. Seven, if he counted the one who'd gone outside. Carefully, Bolan picked his way across the gantry, trying to get a view of the office. He could hear a raised voice coming from within.

Bolan set the UMP on the gantry rail, bracing it. Then he slowly unclipped several smoke grenades and two M84 stun grenades and set them down beside him, in a line. Five grenades would help to even the odds, if used correctly. But his targets were too clumped together. Normally, that wouldn't be a problem, but Ackroyd was in the line of fire. Bolan needed to separate Ackroyd from his watchdogs. The Executioner swept his gaze across the warehouse, hunting. When he found what he was looking for, he crouch-walked across the gantry and removed one of a trio of throwing knives sheathed on his combat harness.

The flat, balanced blades were heavy enough not to result in bounce-back, but light enough that a man of Bolan's strength could send them hurtling a great distance. The knives had been crafted by Stony Man's own weaponsmith, John "Cowboy" Kissinger, according to Bolan's specifications. While Bolan preferred his KA-BAR combat knife, there were times the lighter knives came in handy.

He took aim at the control panel for the conveyor belt. Then, with a whip-crack motion of one arm, the Executioner sent the blade spinning at the panel. It struck a wide button and with a grinding squeal, the conveyer belt rumbled into motion. Bolan quickly made his way back to his grenades. He stuck earplugs into his ears and placed a mouth guard between his teeth. Then he pulled a pair of tinted safety glasses from a pocket and put them on. Between the plugs and the glasses, he would be protected from his own handiwork.

Down below, the sudden activation of the conveyer had startled Ackroyd's guards into motion. Sparrow peered out of the office, a cell phone in one hand. The three men who headed for the belt held their weapons loosely. An overconfident bunch, they clearly weren't expecting an attack. Bolan clucked his tongue and gently lobbed a smoke grenade at the far-loading dock. Pulling the pin on a second, he dropped it from the gantry onto the moving conveyor belt. A second later, he sent the last wobbling through the air straight for the picnic tables. Then, snatching up the stun grenades in one hand, he dropped from the gantry to the top of the conveyer belt. He landed hard and bent his knees, propelling himself forward onto his belly. Lying flat, Bolan slid down the incline of the conveyer belt as the warehouse filled with smoke.

It was a risky maneuver, but it was the best one available to him. As the old maxim said, "when in doubt, attack."

Bolan rode the belt between the two spreading clouds of smoke, his UMP at the ready. As he caught sight of the confused guards hurrying away from the picnic tables, he popped the pin on one of the M84s and sent the bomb hurtling at the small group.

The stun grenade emitted a blinding flash and a bang of 170 decibels—loud enough to cause temporary deafness and ringing in the ears. Despite his safety glasses, Bolan kept his eyes shut and covered his ears as the grenade went off. He didn't open them until he'd rolled off the conveyer belt and hit the floor. Bolan raised his UMP as he came to his feet. He let off a short burst and the three men did a deathly jitterbug as the rounds shredded their bodies. Bolan spun toward the picnic tables and let off another burst, taking out a fourth gunman, who'd been running forward when the grenade had gone off.

Slowly, the Executioner stalked through the warehouse. The stun grenade should have flattened everyone, or at least disorientated them. A shape staggered through the smoke, clutching a rifle. Bolan waited for it to draw closer. One of the guards, coughing, obviously deafened. He stared blurrily at Bolan, and comprehension crept sluggishly into his gaze. He began to raise his weapon and Bolan put him down.

He stepped over the body and headed for Ackroyd,

who was crouching beneath one of the picnic tables. Nearby, a gunman had flipped over another table and was using it as cover. When he caught sight of Bolan, he let loose a burst from his AR-15. Bolan reacted with almost-feline agility, darting to the side as bullets chewed the concrete floor. He twisted midsprint, spraying the overturned table. As he did so, he saw Ackroyd mouth something. The old man's eyes were wide and full of warning.

More shots cut toward him from the other side of the building, and Bolan saw the seventh man crouched behind the conveyer belt. He'd obviously heard the gunfire and cut his smoke break short. The Executioner thumbed the pin out of the remaining M84 and sent the grenade sailing right at the seventh man with an underhand lob. Bolan threw himself flat. The stun grenade went off with a burst of pyrotechnics, igniting the gasoline fumes on the loading dock and triggering a fiery explosion.

The seventh man disintegrated in the blast and Bolan was sent skidding across the floor. The UMP clattered from his grip as he rolled across the concrete with bone-bruising velocity. His back smashed against one of the soda machines and it fell on top of him, pinning him to the floor. A moment later, the second toppled across the first and the ember of pain that had begun to flicker in the back of Bolan's skull exploded into blazing incandescence. Fire alarms began to blare and somewhere above, the warehouse's sprinkler system activated. Water splashed down in sheets, stinging Bolan's eyes and face. Black, oily smoke mingled with the lighter variety from the M84s and Bolan began to cough. He shoved at one of the pop machines, trying to shift it. It rocked slightly, and the pressure on his legs eased. If he could raise it high enough, he might be able to slide his legs out. A sound caused Bolan to look up from his exertions.

Through the greasy coils of smoke that were rapidly filling the warehouse, the remaining gunman approached with his pistol extended. *"Vril-YA!"* The man coughed and took aim.

The Executioner reacted with deadly precision. Even as the gunman's finger tightened on the trigger, Bolan snatched at one of his remaining throwing knives and whipped it forward with lethal accuracy. The knife seemed to sprout from the gunman's skull and he crumpled without a sound, the pistol going off harmlessly as he fell.

Bolan immediately went back to shifting the soda machines. The smoke clawed at his lungs and seared his sinuses as it spread through the warehouse. Even with the sprinklers pounding down, the fire didn't seem to be going out. He needed to grab Ackroyd and get out of the warehouse fast. The building might not burn down, but it would become a veritable oven— they'd cook if they didn't smother. He shoved at the soda machine, trying to get his hands under it.

"Well, ain't this a kick to the pine nuts?" Bolan looked up and saw the hunched shape of Ackroyd making his way through the smoke. "You still alive, kid?"

"Hardly a kid," Bolan said as he tried to work his shoulder up under the machine. His body was starting to throb with agony, and his contortions weren't helping matters. "Name's Cooper. I'm with the Justice Department," he said, giving Ackroyd one of his cover names.

"Younger than me," Ackroyd said, "and I figured." He coughed and glared at the smoke as if it had personally offended him. "You made a real mess of things, kid."

"I'll apologize later. We need to get out of here," Bolan said, wincing as the soda machines settled. It was all a matter of leverage, rather than strength. He had none, so the weight was proving impossible to budge. "If you can find something to help me lever this thing up…"

"I can't," Ackroyd said, looking at him helplessly.

"Anything at all," Bolan insisted. "Grab one of those benches and drag it over here…"

"You ain't hearing me, son. I can't." Suddenly, the sprinkler system cut off.

"No, old man, you can't," Sparrow said, stepping into Bolan's field of view. He had a pistol in his hand, but it wasn't pointed anywhere in particular. That didn't make Bolan feel any better. Sparrow looked down at the man Bolan had taken out with the throwing knife and sighed heavily. "Poor Alexi," he murmured. His gaze swung back to Bolan and turned vicious. "You," he growled. The pistol rose.

Ackroyd stepped between them. "No," the old man said.

"Out of the way," Sparrow snapped.

"I won't let you murder a man in front of me," Ackroyd rasped. "You might have me over a barrel— you've got guns on my family and I have to get you into HYPERBOREA—but you'll have to kill me stone dead before I let you shoot a man in cold blood in front of me."

Bolan tensed. Surreptitiously, he began to reach for his remaining throwing knife. If he could get it out quickly enough, he might be able to take out Sparrow. He never got the chance to try, however. Sparrow shoved the old man out of the way and delivered a hard kick to Bolan's skull. Stars burst and flared before his eyes as pain ripped through his head. Dizzy, Bolan slumped back and groaned as the machines settled more firmly atop him.

"Fine," Sparrow snarled. "I won't kill him. But he'll die all the same. Mervin wanted us to burn this place and the fire this fool started will do just that. No witnesses, no evidence." He looked down at Bolan. "A few minutes of hell don't make up for the men you killed, but it'll do."

Bolan spat blood and tried to raise his head, but a wave of dizziness overwhelmed him. Sparrow turned and grabbed Ackroyd. Through blurred vision, the Executioner watched as the man he'd come to rescue was snatched out of reach yet again.

6

Bolan's throat burned and his sinuses felt as if they'd been swabbed out with barbed wire. With the sprinkler system turned off, the fire had grown in strength, and the building was rapidly filling with smoke. As he groaned and tried to raise his head, something in the back of the warehouse exploded, adding smoke to the spreading inferno. He coughed raggedly. It was getting hard to breathe and he felt like an overcooked sausage, ready to burst. With a primal instinct, Bolan knew that to stay where he was meant certain death.

He shook his head, trying to clear it. Sparrow must have cut off the sprinklers. A gutted warehouse meant no evidence, and that implied there was evidence to be found. He looked around, trying to focus. Adrenaline surged through him and, bracing one forearm against the soda machine, he gave a bone-twisting heave and forced it up. Shattered plastic and burst cans tumbled across him, splattering him with stickiness. With a groan, Bolan caught the edge of the machine with his other hand. He dragged his aching legs up toward his chest. Plastic shards tore through his fatigues and a curse slipped through his clenched teeth. Balancing the weight on his forearms and knees, he took a mo-

ment to catch his breath. Then, in a burst of strength
that few other men could match, Bolan gave a heave
and sent the soda machines toppling off him. He gave
a groan of relief as the pressure that had been steadily
crushing his chest and lungs vanished.

His body ached from the crown of his head to the
soles of his feet. Nonetheless, Bolan rolled onto his
stomach and shoved himself to his feet. He staggered
to the office, leaned against the doorframe and tried to
catch his breath. Sparrow had set a fire in the waste-
basket. Bolan caught sight of what he recognized as
plane tickets and snatched them out of the flames,
whipping them through the air to extinguish them.
He could just make out the name of the departure and
arrival locations. Stuffing the charred tickets into a
pocket, he picked up the phone to call the fire department. Then, after a last look around, Bolan made his
way to his own vehicle. As he shot down the road,
a number of fire trucks blazed past, sirens wailing.
Bolan allowed himself a brief moment of triumph. If
Sparrow wanted the place burned, that was reason
enough for Bolan to make sure it wasn't.

SOMETIME LATER, THE Executioner arrived at the Reno-
Tahoe International Airport. On the way over, he'd
called Stony Man Farm and given Kurtzman the information he'd recovered from the office. Now Bolan
was parked in the long-stay parking lot of the airport,
considering his next move.

Reno-Tahoe was one of the busiest airports in the
nation, and as such, it had the increased security presence now common to all such airports. Even so, Sparrow's plan was clever—a commercial flight would be

harder to divert and harder to control than a private flight. There would be plenty of innocent bystanders, and Ackroyd's good behavior was guaranteed.

Still eyeing the airport, Bolan reached over onto the seat beside him and hefted his phone. He rang up Stony Man Farm to see if Kurtzman had gotten his information. Brognola answered. Tersely, Bolan told Brognola what he'd learned, including what Ackroyd had said about his family. Brognola cursed virulently. The big Fed's own family had come under fire once, and the memory stung a nerve.

"I'll get our people on it. I'm still getting the cold shoulder regarding Ackroyd's files, but I'm more than willing to shove their need-to-know right up their posteriors rather than let one civilian suffer," Brognola snarled. Bolan could picture the older man chomping on one of his cigars as he spoke. "Here, talk to Aaron. I've got some asses to kick," he added.

Abruptly, the line switched over and Aaron Kurtzman said, "Striker? I got the info you requested, but first—I found out who you're up against this go-round."

"Wonderful," Bolan said. "Who are they?"

"They're Nazis," Kurtzman replied flatly. "And not just that—they're a full-blown apocalyptic cult."

"Meaning?" Bolan asked.

"The Society of Thylea was a group of German occultists who got together in Munich after the First World War. The membership list reads like a Who's Who of early Nazi sympathizers. They believed the Aryan race was descended from the peoples of the lost continent of Atlantis, and they think that bringing this world to an end will resurrect the empire of Atlantis."

Bolan blinked. "Atlantis," he repeated.

"As in 'The Man from…' starring Patrick Duffy. A lost civilization with advanced technology. Remember your pal Bulwer-Lytton?" Kurtzman asked.

"Vril," Bolan replied, catching the reference. He pinched the bridge of his nose. "Great."

"Oh, you don't know the half of it. These guys are all over the Net, Striker. They're like slugs, leaving a slime trail across everything. And they've got serious money behind them. It looks like the Society funds half a dozen white-power groups in the good old US of A and twice that number in Europe. That warehouse they were in? That was one of theirs. SunCo, Kohson, T.H. Lea and Sons, and four or five more shell companies scattered across the continental United States. They're like ticks with their teeth sunk into a dog. They advocate race war, ethnic cleansing and a host of other unpleasant things. And they're funding separatist groups in Spain, Greece and several other countries. Lately they've developed an unhealthy focus on a phantom called HYPERBOREA."

Alarm bells went off in Bolan's head. "Ackroyd mentioned that name. What is it?" He began to suspect he knew why Brognola's investigation was being blocked.

"A ghost, like I said. According to the Feds, it doesn't exist. But whatever HYPERBOREA is, it looks like the Society of Thylea thinks they've found it. And that spells bad news, I'd wager." Kurtzman sighed. "I'm still digging, but we're getting stonewalled. I'm guessing it's something that everyone in the know wants to stay buried. How this bunch of nutter-butters found out about it, I can't say, but it'd probably be for the best if they didn't get their hands on it."

Bolan shook his head absently, processing what Kurtzman had told him. "They're fanatics," he said, finally. "It doesn't matter whether they're praying to Allah, Jehovah or Odin. They need to be put down—and *hard*."

"There are tickets waiting for you at the Alaskan Airlines counter, Striker," Kurtzman said. "We found the flight they're on, thanks to the information you recovered from the warehouse, and we got you a seat. The flight's packed, but there's an air marshal on board. They'll be waiting for you and will get you on."

Bolan almost protested. Every fiber of his being demanded that he bring down his quarry then and there, before he left Reno, but Bolan knew that caution was required, especially if Ackroyd's family was under the guns of whoever Sparrow was working for. There was no guarantee that Sparrow's progress wasn't being observed, and if he failed to show up in Seattle, Ackroyd's family might pay the price.

"And when we land at Seattle, I'll take him," Bolan said harshly. "Then we'll find out what's going on. Ask Hal to meet me in Seattle, if he can. I have a feeling we're going to need every marker he can call in on this one."

"Good luck, Striker," Kurtzman said. Bolan ended the call and made a sound of disgust. This wasn't the first time he'd run up against walls built from bricks of bureaucratic silence. Indeed, though he didn't like to think of it that way, he owed his life to one such situation. If not for Hal Brognola and his supporters in the government, the Executioner would not have gotten a second chance to continue his war.

But in this case, someone, somewhere, was willing to endanger a lot of lives to keep their dirty little secret, and Bolan had no time for such cowardice. Bolan trusted Brognola to protect Ackroyd's family. It was up to the Executioner to take care of the rest.

When Bolan arrived at check-in, he made his way to the Alaskan Airlines counter. He'd taken the time to quickly change from his scorched and torn fatigues into his civvies, and he'd left his weapons in the car, save for the Desert Eagle which was snugly holstered beneath his arm, its bulk hidden by the hang of the battered denim jacket he wore over his T-shirt. At any other time, in any other situation, he wouldn't have brought the weapon into the airport, but as Kurtzman had promised, they were expecting him.

The men and women behind the counter looked alternately nervous and excited as he approached. One of the women stepped out from behind the counter as Bolan walked up and said, "Right this way, Mr. Cooper." He followed her through a door marked AUTHORIZED PERSONNEL ONLY and down a back corridor. As they walked, she snuck quick looks at the shape of the Desert Eagle, but she said nothing.

She led him to a room where a number of security personnel stood around a bank of video monitors. One of the security staff—a tall African-American man dressed in a dark suit—turned to greet Bolan. He smiled flatly and introduced himself. "Alvarez, Federal Air Marshal Service. You're Cooper, right?" His eyes strayed to the holstered pistol, but, as with Bolan's guide, he said nothing.

"If I wasn't, would I be here?" Bolan asked.

"Depends," Alvarez replied. "We once had a delivery man get back here by accident. Poor guy was determined to deliver that pizza, even after we got him into custody."

"I'm Cooper," Bolan said, smiling slightly.

The two men shook hands and Alvarez indicated the monitors. "Your guy—Sparrow, was it?—he's gone through security and he's in the concourse now, with his pal. We were told you didn't want us to stop him." Bolan caught the implied accusation, but couldn't find it in him to blame Alvarez. There wasn't a security man in the world that didn't bristle at the thought of his routine being disrupted. Routine meant everything was going well. Routine meant that everyone was safe. When routine got screwed, so did the security man on whose watch it happened.

Bolan peered at the monitor. "No. We have reason to believe that to do so will result in the deaths of several people."

"Old man's under duress," Alvarez said. Bolan looked at him. Alvarez rubbed his face tiredly. "I've been with the Federal Air Marshal Service for almost twenty years, Cooper. I've seen my share of forced transports—usually it's kids or women—and I know when someone is being forced to go somewhere they'd rather not." He tapped one of the monitors for emphasis.

"His family," Bolan said quietly. "We've got people on it, but there are no guarantees…"

Alvarez grunted. "Figures," he said. "But you're planning on taking him in Seattle?"

"If possible."

"Okay." Alvarez gestured to the Desert Eagle. "I hope you're not planning on taking that cannon on board. Justice Department or not, I can't risk it."

Bolan bristled, but only for a moment. Sparrow wouldn't be armed, either. He nodded. "Understood."

"I, however, will be armed," Alvarez said, smiling thinly. He caught Bolan's expression and said, "You didn't think I was letting some Justice Department cowboy on one of my planes unescorted, did you?"

Bolan crossed his arms. "I'm not complaining," he said. "A little backup never hurt anyone."

"Surprisingly reasonable of you—you sure you work for the Justice Department, Cooper?" Bolan smiled and slipped the Desert Eagle out of its holster.

He ejected the magazine and then ejected the round in the chamber, deftly catching the bullet as it arced through the air. Alvarez's eyes widened slightly. Bolan set pistol, magazine and bullet down on the table. Then, still smiling, he looked at Alvarez.

"Let's go. I don't want to miss my flight."

7

Anchorage, Alaska

Kraft sat on the edge of the bed, humming softly, while Mervin talked at length with Sparrow, who'd made the mistake of calling from the Reno airport to report that Mervin's delicate plans had once again been disrupted. Kraft, no stranger to Mervin's tantrums, felt some sympathy for Sparrow, but not much.

Sparrow was a good soldier, but he was also a mongrel, as all Americans were. That meant he couldn't be trusted with even the simplest tasks without supervision. Mervin did not recognize the part purity of blood played in how men acted and reacted. Pure Aryans would have dealt efficiently and permanently with the interfering party. But if Mervin could not see it, he did not consider it.

Kraft pitied him. He was a bright young man, with a mind that was obviously at one with the *Vril*—the secret life-blood of the universe. But his body—his poor, impure body—was not of the proper stock to handle the god-mind of the soon-to-come ancient Thylea.

Kraft looked at his hands. The tanned flesh was as

hard as leather and marred by hundreds of thin scars of varying sizes and shapes. His fingers curled inward and his knuckles popped like gunshots. Mervin glanced at him, startled. Kraft smiled. Mervin went back to berating Sparrow in his calm, monotone way.

Kraft knew he was of the proper stock. Had not his father and grandfather and great-grandfather served the Society of Thylea, even as he did? From the very beginning, the Krafts had served as the strong hands that did the work of kings. They were of the blood of the paladins of old, who had built empires, pale shadows of lost Thylea, to better mankind.

That dream was the reason Kraft had given up his rank and left the military to take up his father's post as castellan of the Society. He was the strong shield that, together with their sword, would enact the vast and far-reaching plans of the Sun-Koh. The Society's ruling council was scattered across Europe, from Moscow to Vienna to Milan. They were men of wisdom and power, who rarely met in person, preferring to speak as electronic phantoms in locked and hidden places on the internet. Kraft never had much time for computers himself. If he could not touch it or break it, he distrusted it. But like a good soldier—like a true warrior—he recognized his own failings and trusted his fellow paladins, like Mervin, to take up the slack.

Mervin tossed the satellite phone onto the bed. "Fool," he said.

Kraft looked up.

"Not you. Sparrow."

"I know," Kraft said, picking up the phone and placing it carefully back on the desk. "More interference, I take it?"

"The same interference, if Sparrow is to be believed."

"You doubt him?"

Mervin hesitated. "No. Once is coincidence. Twice is enemy action."

It was Kraft's turn to hesitate. "Should we abort the mission?"

"That would solve nothing. We are committed. We must continue." Mervin's voice was as flat as ever, but there was an edge to it that Kraft found gratifying. He occasionally wondered about Mervin's dedication to their cause. It was good that he, too, seemed to feel what Kraft felt. This was destiny, and destiny could not be denied.

"As you say," Kraft agreed. He slapped his knees and rose to his feet. "Where is Sparrow now?"

"Preparing to board the plane for Seattle," Mervin said, not looking at Kraft. "He will call again, once he has arrived."

"Do we have anyone meeting him?"

"No. There was no need."

"Except now there might be," Kraft chided. It always paid to be gentle with Mervin. "How much interference did he encounter, exactly?"

"Sparrow is alone," Mervin replied, sitting on the bed. His fingers twitched. "The others…?" Kraft asked.

"All dead." Mervin closed his eyes and lay back on the bed, massaging his temples. "One man killed them all. Enemy action," he added.

"One man," Kraft murmured. "Interesting…"

Mervin's eyes cracked open. "No, frustrating," he

corrected. "One man should not have been able to interfere to this extent."

"Never underestimate the power of a single man."

"Irrelevant. The man is dead. Sparrow and the others were lazy. Their methods were lacking. They have endangered my plan. When Sparrow reaches Anchorage, dispense with him."

Kraft frowned. "Why? He is a loyal member of the Society, and he has proven his worth, obviously, by succeeding where the others failed."

"He has not succeeded—merely survived. He is a weak cog, Kraft, and he must be stripped from the machine. We have plenty of soldiers. One more or less will not make a difference. I want to sleep before we go to the airport."

Kraft grunted. "You want to smoke one of your filthy cigarettes, you mean."

Mervin didn't reply. Kraft sighed and left the room. He closed the door quietly behind him and stood in the hotel hallway for a moment, considering. Mervin had a room to himself, mostly because no one else could stand to bunk with him for any length of time. Even Kraft's dedication only went so far. He had no illusions as to Mervin's personality. While his mind was a valuable weapon in the Society's war with the lesser races, Mervin himself was a nasty little creature. He was spiteful, brusque and petulant. He smoked like a chimney and seemed to subsist entirely on ego and nicotine.

He was not a warrior. Kraft, however, was. He had been a warrior even before he'd been trained to use those instincts. And now he was one of the most dangerous killers the world had ever seen. He had killed

Interpol agents and MI6 gunmen in his time. He'd
fought jihadists and anarchists, *Vory* killers and, once,
a Yakuza assassin, covered in tattoos and wearing a
mask like the devil's face. That one he had fought
amongst the electric pastel stars that lit up the Shin-
juku district of Tokyo, and he still had the long, thin
scars to remember their lethal dance.

For Kraft, battle was meat and drink. He longed
for the scream of bullets sawing through the red mist
and the hiss-thud-whack of steel on flesh. He closed
his eyes, imagining it. And then he thought of the unknown interferer. He wondered what the man's name
was and whether he was truly dead. Sparrow was
competent, but was he competent enough to take out
a man who had killed so many of their own? Kraft
doubted it.

He felt heartened by the thought. Kraft had been
too long without a challenge. He wanted the man,
whoever he was, to have survived. If he lived, he
would keep coming after Sparrow, after them. Kraft
felt it in his bones. He sensed that this man was a fellow warrior. The thought brought a smile to his face.
It would be good to meet a worthy foe one last time,
before the world ended and began anew.

Kraft flexed his fingers, imagining them sinking into his faceless enemy's flesh. Then, decided,
he moved noiselessly down the hall toward the room
he shared with one of the others, a Canadian named
Boyd. In the room, Boyd and several of the other men
were sitting on the beds, drinking beer, eating pizza
and assembling their weapons. The AR-15s had been
cheap and easy to acquire, and the handguns, as well.
The weapons had been waiting for them at a SunCo

subsidiary in Anchorage, labelled as "pest control." Which, in a sense, they were, he mused.

For a moment, he examined the group. A feeling of pride filled him. They were of varied backgrounds—some had been soldiers and others, like Boyd, had been petty criminals before finding the Society. But they had all come together, united by a common, glorious goal. "Sparrow made it to the airport," Kraft said, shutting the door behind him.

"Did you doubt it?" Boyd asked as he dropped a pepperoni into his mouth.

"There's been interference."

Suddenly, every eye was on him, as he'd intended. Despite Mervin's assertions to the contrary, Kraft knew that his men were the equal to most global military organizations. He had trained them himself. Boyd, chewing, asked, "How many?"

"One, according to Sparrow," Kraft said.

Boyd sniffed. A soft mutter arose from the gathered men. Kraft raised a hand. "Quietly, gentlemen," he said.

"What does the Tick-Tock Man say?" Boyd asked. Kraft gave him a baleful look. Boyd ignored it. Kraft usually gave him more leeway than the others. Boyd was good for morale, being quick-witted and good with a joke. Sometimes, however, he pushed his luck too far.

At times like that, Kraft was forced to discipline him. Kraft moved smoothly across the small distance between them, one long arm unfolding. His hand clamped around Boyd's windpipe and he jerked the Canadian up and swung him around, smashing him against the wall in one forceful motion. Boyd's face turned red as Kraft examined him for a moment and then turned his cold gaze onto the rest of the men. "Do not insult Mervin. When you insult Mervin, when you mock him, you mock the Society. You mock the men who have raised us up and placed their trust in a vessel you deem unworthy. Who are you to determine worthiness?"

Having said his piece, he let Boyd drop. The Canadian bent double and wheezed. He rubbed his throat, looked up at Kraft and rasped, "Made—made me swallow a pepperoni."

A ripple of amusement punctured the tension. Kraft smiled and patted Boyd on the back. "I apologize. Have another slice, please." He gestured to the pizza box on the bed. "One man, gentlemen," he continued. "A singular man. Mervin has dismissed him already. We will not. Sparrow says he is dead. Perhaps he is. Mervin certainly believes such to be the case. But Mervin is not a warrior. He does not understand warriors. We are too close to our moment of destiny, my friends. Our enemies gather and in the great, far dark, the *Gjallarhorn* sounds."

Several of his men nodded fiercely at the mention of the war-horn of the god *Heimdallr*. Others looked blank. Not all servants of the Society knew of the old gods. Not all of those who did believed. Kraft did not worry one way or the other. "We are many, and he is one," he said. "But all warriors are alone on the battlefield."

"So who is—was—he?" Boyd asked.

"Unknown," Kraft answered honestly. "He could be a hitter for a rival organization or an operative for one of half a dozen governments. If he is dead, it doesn't matter. Even if he's alive, it doesn't matter. We are on the sharp end, my friends, and every man's hand is against us." He clapped his hands together. "When we reach HYPERBOREA, nothing will matter, save the end."

His men murmured. They did not know everything, for Mervin had seen no reason to tell them. But Kraft was not Mervin. Kraft was a warrior and it befitted warriors to have no secrets. "Yes, you know that name, my friends. And what we will find there is the answer to this sick world. At HYPERBOREA, we will find Thylea…and the world will at last see our power!"

8

Bolan had spotted Sparrow and Ackroyd almost as soon as he'd boarded the Boeing 737. A single aisle ran the length of the cabin, with three seats to the rows to either side. The two men were seated in the middle of the compartment, and Sparrow had Ackroyd boxed in against the window. Bolan was fairly certain that Sparrow had spotted him, as well, if the sickly expression on the other man's face was anything to go by. But Alvarez had passed by unnoticed and was sitting directly behind them. That gave the air marshal an advantage, if Sparrow decided to try something.

If Bolan had been in Sparrow's shoes, he wouldn't have risked making a move on the plane. It was much easier to lose any pursuers in the airport after disembarking. But Sparrow wasn't Bolan, and when Bolan surreptitiously glanced back at the man, he could tell that the pressure was already getting to him.

An hour into the flight, they were closing in on Seattle-Tacoma. The "Fasten Seat Belt" light was on, and the drink carts were being stowed. Sparrow looked like he was about to explode. He'd been getting more and more agitated as the flight progressed.

Bolan wondered what was going through the killer's

mind. His face had taken on a waxy sheen and his eyes were bright with nervousness. Sparrow had no weapons, but he could still be dangerous. Bolan knew of at least six different ways to create a crude weapon aboard a plane. Sparrow probably did, as well.

Bolan met Alvarez's gaze and the other man nodded slightly. Sitting as close as he was, Alvarez could probably tell how nervous Sparrow was getting. When the latter stood abruptly and went to the lavatory at the rear of the plane, the air marshal stood, too, and followed at a discreet pace. Alvarez was sharp. He didn't plan on giving Sparrow an inch of privacy.

A flight attendant tried to block Alvarez, but he said something and her face went pale. Bolan unbuckled his seat belt and stood. Pulling himself along the aisle, his hands gripping the seats, he made his way to Ackroyd. Alvarez could keep Sparrow occupied while Bolan spoke to the old man.

Ackroyd started as Bolan sat down beside him. "You," he said. "But…"

"You saved my life, Dr. Ackroyd, and I intend to return the favor."

"But my family…"

"They'll be fine," Bolan said, squeezing the old man's shoulder. "I've made sure of it. We're going to take Sparrow in Seattle. When it goes down, you need to find cover and fast. Can you do that for me?"

"Son, my cowardly rear was hunting cover before you were born." Ackroyd grabbed Bolan's wrist. "You're sure about my granddaughter? Because if you're not, I'll… I don't know what I'll do," he said, releasing Bolan and slumping back into his seat. The Executioner felt a stab of sympathy. He wanted to say something—anything—comforting, but nothing came to mind. There were some fears words alone could not dispel. Raised voices warned Bolan that Sparrow was done. The Executioner stood quickly, prepared to make his way back to his seat, when the sounds of a commotion drew his attention.

Bolan turned just in time to see Alvarez slump against the lavatory door, shards of glass covering his face. Sparrow had grabbed the coffeepot from its warmer and smashed it across the air marshal's forehead. The flight attendant screamed as Sparrow grabbed her arm and shoved her aside. His fingers curled and the heel of his palm danced across Alvarez's throat with a velocity and force that was just this side of lethal. The air marshal gagged and shuddered and his coat fell open. Sparrow's lips skinned back from his teeth in a feral grimace and he snatched the weapon free of its holster in a surprisingly fluid move.

"I should have shot you in Reno," he shouted as he spotted Bolan.

"You'll forgive me if I disagree," Bolan said, stepping forward. Then, more loudly, "Ladies and gentlemen, please stay in your seats. My name is Matt Cooper and I'm with the Justice Department. Remain in your seats, and we'll have you safe and sound in Seattle in a few minutes."

"Shut up," Sparrow snapped, stalking forward. "Nobody is going anywhere until I say!"

"We'll see about that," Bolan said. He helped the flight attendant to her feet. "I'm guessing this plane has enough fuel for—what—an extra hour of flight time?"

"Just about," she said. The pretty, middle-aged

woman had black hair and refined features, but her eyes were as hard and sharp as kitchen knives as she glared at Sparrow. People often forgot that flight attendants were the last line of defense against those who might try to harm passengers.

Bolan gently moved her behind him then looked back at Sparrow. "So nobody is going anywhere for an hour. Then this plane is either landing or falling. But that's beside the point. You're not in charge here, Sparrow."

Sparrow gnawed his lip. The gun didn't tremble, but he wasn't aiming it anywhere in particular. Bolan wanted to keep it that way. "I have the gun," Sparrow said. He kicked Alvarez, who was sitting on the floor, his face a mess of burns and blood. The air marshal groaned. "And I have a hostage."

"No, what you have is a problem," Bolan said, edging closer. "You're only going to get one shot, and I'm fairly certain you're not good enough to hit me, even this close. If you miss—assuming you don't hit one of the innocent people around us—one of four things will happen." Bolan slid forward another few inches. "One, you'll punch a hole in the plane itself. Not a big deal, really, despite what movies would have you believe."

Sparrow was staring at him with wary fascination, like a rat watching an approaching snake.

"Two, you'll pop a window, which is worse. Someone could get sucked out, and the cabin will be filled with so much flying debris that a concussion will be the least of your worries. That's if the sudden drop in pressure and oxygen doesn't do you in. You're not in your seat, and I'm not planning on handing you an oxygen mask.

"Three, your bullet clips some wiring. You might stop the in-flight entertainment or you could kill the radar or something worse. And four—four is the big one—your shot could puncture one of the fuel tanks. Which, if we're lucky, just causes a fire, but if we're not…" Bolan spread his hands. *"Boom."*

Sparrow hesitated. Then, with a shrug, he said, "I'll risk it."

Bolan, who'd been ready for that response, moved like lightning. As Sparrow took aim, the Executioner grabbed the headrests of the seats on either side of him and swung his legs up, kicking the pistol from Sparrow's grip. Still balancing on the headrests, he then drove both feet into the other man's chest, sending him flying backward down the aisle and into the food area. Bolan dropped to his feet and lunged, fingers curved into hooks. He crashed down onto Sparrow and bounced his opponent's head off the floor.

Sparrow grunted and his fist jabbed pistonlike up into Bolan's solar plexus. Dazed as Sparrow was, there was still plenty of fight left in him. He punched Bolan again and shoved him back. Bolan reeled and then lunged forward again, even as Sparrow got his feet under him. Crouched in the aisle, inches apart, the two men traded vicious blows.

The Executioner caught Sparrow's fist as the latter sent a short, sharp blow on a collision course for Bolan's jaw. Bolan's fingers tightened, vise-like, on Sparrow's hand. Bone creaked and cartilage popped, eliciting a yell from Sparrow, who slumped back, clawing at the hand that held his. Bolan rose to his feet and dragged Sparrow with him. He twisted his opponent's wrist, contorting Sparrow's arm to an unnatural degree. Sparrow howled and jerked, unable to break Bolan's steely grip.

Then, with a finality that reassured the wide-eyed passengers who had watched the fight in stunned silence, Bolan's fist fell across Sparrow's jaw. He went still and Bolan released him, letting him fall to the floor, unconscious.

The pilot, as yet unaware of what had transpired, came on the intercom to announce the flight's arrival at Seattle-Tacoma. Bolan picked up Alvarez's pistol and stuffed it into his waistband as he helped the flight attendant get the air marshal into an empty seat. She retrieved a first-aid kit and began to see to Alvarez's wounds.

"Sorry about that, Cooper," Alvarez croaked. "I thought if I braced him in the john, he might give us less trouble. I figured I could wrap it all up neat and quick."

"Nothing to apologize for," Bolan said. "I might have done the same thing myself, if I'd been sitting where you were."

"You got him, though?"

"We got him," Bolan said. He turned as Ackroyd made his way toward them. "Is there anything I can do?" the old man asked.

"Yeah," Bolan said, straightening up. "You can tell me what this has all been about."

Ackroyd looked startled. "You mean…you don't know?"

"No. This wasn't my game, Dr. Ackroyd. I just

happened to deal myself in. Why did these guys want you?"

"I—I don't know that I can tell you, son," Ackroyd said.

Bolan grunted in exasperation. "You'd better figure it out. I don't like fighting shadows, and I hate when people value secrets over the lives of innocents."

Ackroyd flushed. "You sonnuva—"

Bolan leaned close to the old man. "Probably. God knows I've been called worse. But that doesn't change anything. I need to know what's going on, and I need to know *now*."

9

Seattle-Tacoma International Airport

Hal Brognola was waiting on the tarmac outside the arrival terminal. The passengers had already been ushered off the plane and into the terminal by airport security. The immediate area had been cleared of bystanders and a number of people wearing sunglasses and suits that shouted "Federal agent" now occupied it, looking uncomfortable beneath the open sky. Brognola was chewing on a cigar, his face set in an expression that Bolan rated as being equal parts determination and frustration. The Executioner and the flight attendant helped guide Alvarez down the stairs. The air marshal was swiftly retrieved by a duo of paramedics who had been standing by, and he gave Bolan a thumbs-up as he was loaded into the waiting ambulance.

Bolan stepped aside as several of the suits-and-sunglasses rushed onto the plane to retrieve Sparrow, whom Bolan had handcuffed to a seat. He handed the air marshal's pistol to Brognola after extracting the magazine. "I take it you managed to cut through the red tape," he said drily.

"Not as much as I'd like," Brognola grunted, shoving the weapon into the hands of an agent. "I brought your standby gear, and Kissinger says hello, by the way."

Bolan smiled. If Kissinger had been involved in procuring his replacement weapons, they would be reliable. The smile faded. "What about Ackroyd's family?"

Brognola's expression was stern. "They're safe. We got the gunmen." He shook his head, answering Bolan's next question before the other man could ask it. "They went hard, every mother's son of them. We made them easily enough, but they put up a hell of a fight, and in public. We're spreading the gospel it was a bank robbery gone wrong."

"How many were there?"

Brognola held up three fingers. "They were armed like the ones in Reno. Terrorist-chic, AR-15s. Two of them had records—neo-Nazi skinhead bullshit. The other was English and a member of one of their nationalist parties."

"There was a German in Reno. And a Russian, as well," Bolan said. He scrubbed his chin, thinking. "Kurtzman said this Society of Thylea was global."

"Most terrorist groups are," Brognola pointed out.

He took the cigar out of his mouth and eyed its soggy end speculatively. He tossed it aside with a grunt. "It's a rigged game, Striker."

"Ackroyd intimated as much," Bolan said. "He refused to talk about it…. Said it was classified." He crossed his arms. "I saw that you came with a full complement of civil servants."

"Denizens of the darkest depths of Alphabet City,"

Brognola said. He pulled a new cigar from his breast pocket and carefully peeled off the crinkled plastic wrapper. "DARPA, NSA, FBI and at least one CIA guy, too, though he won't admit it. There are more of them scattered all over this airport. I've got them looking for your playmate's contacts."

"He doesn't have any. This is just a layover," Bolan said. He shook his head. The more government letters that got added to a situation, the more complicated it seemed to get. The men and women who staffed those assorted agencies were competent, but the ever-expanding bureaucracy they were part of was far too stifling. Men and women—good people, effective people—were buried in seas of paperwork and remit, unable to accomplish even the simplest task without filing for permission in triplicate. And those who took no notice of the regulations were either punished or promoted. The latter were usually the wrong ones, in Bolan's estimation.

"I know. I just didn't want them getting under-foot." Brognola stuffed the cigar between his teeth and began masticating it with vigor. Once again, Bolan was reminded of the vast chasm between his sort of battlefield and the arena in which the big Fed fought, and he felt a jolt of relief.

"They're all competing to see who gets to blame the others first," Brognola said. "That group you took out in Reno? They killed an FBI agent, a guy from the Las Vegas office. Frank Ogilvy—he was a Hoover appointment. He was also our Dr. Ackroyd's handler."

"They tortured him," Bolan said. Unfortunately, that was a given, but the mention of Hoover had piqued his curiosity. How old were the secrets that

Ackroyd held? It couldn't be weapons—any weaponry, biological or otherwise, would be so out of date as to be worse than useless. Better to buy something on the black market than go through all this trouble. But Bolan had never been able to fathom the minds of fanatics, and if anyone fit the description, the Society of Thylea seemed to.

"They tortured a lot of people, one after the other, to find the next name on whatever list they're working off. They're determined, Striker, and they've left a lot of human wreckage to get to this point."

"All to find him," Bolan said. An agent hustled Ackroyd off the plane. Bolan moved quickly, intercepting them, and Brognola hurried after.

"Cooper!" Ackroyd burst out as he spotted Bolan. "My family—are they...?"

"Safe," Bolan said. Ackroyd sagged in relief.

"Out of the way," the agent snapped. "This man's in protective custody—"

"Yes, mine." The Executioner's tone brooked no argument, but the other man was either oblivious or brave. He matched Bolan's serene gaze with his own hairy eyeball and reached out as if to push Bolan aside.

"Look, pal, I don't know who you are, but—" the agent began. His face flushed beneath his government regulation haircut as Brognola grabbed his hand a fingertip's width from the Executioner's shoulder and tossed it aside. Before the man could react, Brognola thrust himself forward, and his index finger jack-hammered the agent's chest as he spoke.

"This? This, son, is Agent Matt Cooper, Justice Department. And me, well, you already know me, because I'm the man who got your boss out of bed,"

Brognola snarled. The agent took an instinctive step back, trying to escape the finger. "Now, seeing as Agent Cooper has, to this point, been the only damn one of us to actually be involved in this situation, maybe you could see fit to turn Dr. Ackroyd over, hmm?"

Despite the torrent of authority, the agent still made to reply. But his mouth clamped shut as a new voice intervened. "Ease off, Jenkins." Bolan turned and saw an African-American man walking toward them across the tarmac. He was of an age with Brognola, and he had the hard, square features of someone who'd spent a lifetime in interrogation rooms, drinking coffee until his blood was likely coffee-brown rather than cherry-red. His close-cropped hair was gray and his suit was off-the-rack. "Agent Cooper, I'm Ferguson, FBI."

"Las Vegas branch office?" Bolan hazarded a guess.

Ferguson's chin dipped. "Ogilvy was one of mine."

"I'm sorry," Bolan said.

"He was an ass." Ferguson held out a hand to Ackroyd. "Dr. Ackroyd, good to see you again."

"Frank's really dead?" Ackroyd asked.

"Yes," Ferguson replied.

Ackroyd shook his head. "Hell. I need a cigarette. I need a pack of cigarettes." He looked at Bolan. "Make it two packs."

"I'll buy you a carton as soon as you tell me what I need to know," Bolan said harshly. The Executioner's almost inhuman patience was being tested.

"Hal," Ferguson said, "I told you over the phone—this thing isn't some hush-hush operation you can just bully your way into. It's been classified for close to fifty years."

"Then it makes sense to air it out a bit, don't you think?" Bolan asked.

"It's not up to me," Ferguson said. He sounded resigned.

"Sounds like it's not up to anybody," Bolan said softly. He'd seen this type of situation before—somewhere, at some time, the responsibility for HYPERBOREA had passed into the labyrinthine corridors of the U.S. bureaucracy and disappeared. No one was quite sure, and no one wanted to take responsibility just in case it blew up in their faces. Just another game of CYA—cover your ass—Bolan thought.

Ferguson didn't reply, but Ackroyd made a sound. It took Bolan a few moments to realize that he was laughing. It wasn't a happy sound. Bolan was reminded of the caw of an old crow.

Ackroyd looked up and said, "God Almighty, I should have known." He took off his glasses and rubbed them on his shirt, shaking his head all the while. "I knew it would come to this. The day we found it, the day we lost…" He trailed off. Then he said, "Yeah, hell with it."

"Doctor," Ferguson began, but his warning was halfhearted. Bolan wondered for a moment whether the FBI man had hoped this would happen. Bolan glanced at Brognola and saw that the big Fed had a knowing look in his eye. Brognola and Bolan both knew what it was like to lose a man in the line of duty; Ferguson wouldn't have been human if he hadn't wanted payback, his opinion of Ogilvy notwithstanding.

"No," Ackroyd said. He looked directly at Bolan,

his gaze steady. "I'll tell you everything, Presidential Directive be damned."

Ferguson threw up his hands. "I can't hear this. In fact, we can't be doing this out here." Despite his words, Bolan noticed he was grinning.

"Find us an office, then," the Executioner said. "Dr. Ackroyd and I have several things to discuss."

Ferguson complied, and swiftly enough that Bolan knew for certain the agent had been expecting this. Fifty years was too long to keep a secret. Ackroyd seemed to feel the same way—he started talking as soon as they were alone and Bolan had closed the door.

"It's not a weapon. I know that's what you're thinking, but it's not," Ackroyd said. The old man hunched forward, his fingers intertwining nervously. "It's not a weapon. It's too dangerous for that, frankly."

"Then what is it?" Bolan asked.

"It's death. Pure, concentrated death," Ackroyd said softly. He closed his eyes. "I wasn't just a biologist. My specialty was paleobiology. You know what that is?"

"Like paleontology?"

"That's bones," Ackroyd said. "I dealt with the things that didn't have bones—single-celled organisms, mostly, and—ah—microbacteria. Vinson dealt with the bones." His eyes opened. "We found it in the rocks or under them, rather, up near Noatak, in Alaska. There was a mud shelf, perfectly preserved. Traces of plant life, some bits of decayed animal matter." He paused, and then elaborated, "and by animal matter I mean a body."

"A human body?" Bolan asked.

"An ice mummy," Ackroyd said. He snorted. "A government survey team found it. It was curled up in a ball, preserved in the mud and ice. We'd never found one that close to the Arctic before. Like a baby waiting to be born. There were plenty of microbacteria in that husk. We thought it was the biggest find of the century. Nobel Prizes all around." He smiled bitterly. "What we found was what Vinson—a Norwegian—dubbed *Ymir*—the Ur-plague. Cooper, you know what 'Ur' means?"

"It was one of the first cities," Bolan said. He felt a glimmer of satisfaction as Ackroyd looked at him in surprise. The old man smiled weakly.

"Yeah, that's right. Legend has it that Ur was the city at the mouth of the Euphrates from which all other cities sprang. And Ymir is—was—the first global pandemic, we thought. Still think, to be honest," Ackroyd said. "It was the great-granddaddy of the Black Plague, the first swing of God's own scythe. All the others came from it, the way the giants of Norse mythology all descended from Ymir. And we dug it up, warmed its bones—literally—and almost let it loose…" The old man trailed off, and his gaze went glassy, as if he were looking back into the past, lost in his own memories.

Bolan didn't even try and imagine what Ackroyd was seeing at that moment. He'd witnessed enough in his life that he didn't need to picture specifics. Terror, blood and a creeping dread, as the realization of their own mortality set in. Ackroyd coughed and blinked then continued, "Vinson died. A couple of the others did, as well, before we realized what we were dealing with. The progression from initial infection to full-blown symptoms to becoming contagious is…terrifyingly rapid. A few hours and you're a biological hazard. Twenty-four hours after that…" He gestured helplessly. "We were lucky that it wasn't exactly a subtle bastard. If you had it, you could tell pretty quickly. It was just so damn fast there wasn't much that could be done. We'd woken a demon, and there was no King Solomon around to stick it into a bottle." Ackroyd looked at Bolan, and his eyes were full of agony. "It shouldn't have still been viable. But somehow, it was. And it was hungry after so long in that ice." The old man blinked back tears. He licked his lips. His voice had gone hoarse. "In the end, we managed to contain it. We quarantined the infected. When they…succumbed, we locked it all down. We had to burn everything that wasn't sealed up—clothes, notes and equipment."

"And HYPERBOREA," Bolan pressed.

"We left it. It wasn't on any maps, and it was too far out in the wild for anyone to bother with. Or at least it was back then. I recommended that we sink it—damn thing was basically a repurposed oil rig from the pipeline, you know, and situated right on an isolated tributary of the Noatak River. I told them to blow up the supports and let the base sink down into the water basin, taking Ymir with it. But they didn't. I don't know why."

"Waste not, want not," Bolan said softly.

Ackroyd looked at him sharply. Then, grudgingly, he nodded. "Probably. Even then, there was talk about trying to turn it into a weapon. We were among the best and brightest brains America had, and we were in a theoretical arms race with the Reds—space flight, archaeology, it was all the same to the boys on the Potomac, just one more knife in the bear's hide. The only reason we were out there was to thumb our noses at them. Nobody was supposed to have anything that close to international territory, but if they had raised the alarm about us, we would've known they were out there, as well. But it wasn't the Reds who woke up Ymir. It was us. There's no way that thing can be turned into a useable weapon. It's too virulent. But if it gets out, if it spreads south…"

"What's your best guess?" Bolan asked.

"Sixty, seventy percent of the people on this planet will be dead inside a month." Ackroyd said it flatly, and Bolan knew it was no guess. Ackroyd had calculated those figures over and over since he'd left HYPERBOREA. Every day, the old man's mind had delved into the monstrous mathematics of a global pandemic. Every day, he had charted new maps of Hell.

"That's what they want, you know," he added. He grabbed Bolan's wrist in a surprisingly strong grip. "They don't want to control it. Those men are suicide bombers. They want to let it out and then they'll carry it south and east and west because they're xenophobic, self-aggrandizing assholes who think it's part of some Nazi prophecy and all the good white folks will be spared. But it'll spread and it'll mutate as it spreads— because that's what viruses do—and melanin content or geographic genetic markers won't make a damn bit of difference. As a species, we've evolved past needing whatever antibodies our ancestors developed to fight it, and we'll pay for that in fire and blood. It'll kill us, Cooper. It'll scour the Earth like a Biblical plague, and whoever survives won't be in any shape to set up a new society, Thylea or otherwise."

Bolan had no reply. In all the years of his War Everlasting, very rarely had he faced a threat of such magnitude. It seemed inconceivable, and the sheer weight of it all settled heavily on his shoulders. Grimly, with every iota of will that was his to call upon, Bolan thrust the horror of it aside. Death was death, whether one man's life was at stake or millions, and it was the Executioner's duty to bring justice to the dealers of death.

"You have to stop them, Cooper," Ackroyd said.

"I will," the Executioner replied. He stood. "One way or another, I will."

10

Brognola and Ferguson were waiting for him out in the corridor. "Nasty, ain't it?" the latter said. Bolan looked at him. Ferguson held up his hands. "I know, I know, but you've got to understand, once something has been denied long enough, a sort of gridlock develops. No one wants to talk about it or take responsibility, because it could blow wide open. Every time a bit of space debris gets too close or this season's bird flu mutates, people go nuts. They panic. And we have to run around taking care of that panic."

"CYA," Brognola supplied.

Ferguson shrugged. "What do you want me to do, Hal? Frankly, it was hard enough keeping Ackroyd in what amounted to unofficial witness protection. We did it for all of them, all of the survivors. Set them up for life, wherever they wanted to go. Ackroyd wanted to live somewhere hot."

"Your unofficial witness protection didn't seem to do them much good," Bolan said. It came out more harshly than he'd intended, but Ferguson didn't flinch.

"No, it didn't. Which is why I passed a mash note to Hal as soon as we got wind of something going on," he said.

It made sense in retrospect, Bolan thought. Who else would have known to leak information to Brognola but the one man who had the full picture?

"No one wants to ask the questions they'd have to ask if I had authorized an official response. No one wants to deal with this, Cooper. They just want it to go away." He looked unblinkingly at the Executioner.

Bolan felt his opinion of the man curdling. "You want me to do your dirty work."

"Isn't that why you're here? There's dirty work that needs doing, so you do it," Ferguson said. "I don't care why these assholes want HYPERBOREA. 'Why' is irrelevant. I just want them stopped."

Brognola held up a hand. "We all want them stopped. But I have a feeling we're running low on time. Everything about this has been set to a schedule—regular phone calls, credit transactions, everything."

"Which means we need to find out what the schedule is and what's next on the list," Bolan said. His eyes narrowed. "Where's Sparrow?"

"We've got him in another office. We're waiting for a trained interrogator…." Ferguson said.

"You've got one. Take me to him." Ferguson hesitated. Bolan could practically see his thoughts. "I'm not going to torture him," he said quietly. "But I can get him to talk. And we need him to talk now."

Ferguson grunted. "Yeah," he said. He scratched his cheek and added, "Come on."

There were two agents guarding the office when they arrived. Bolan had taken the time to grab his KA-BAR combat knife as well as the files on Ogilvy's murder—which Ferguson had willingly provided—and the newly arrived dossiers from several of Brognola's European contacts. He'd scanned them all quickly on the walk, picking out the important points. Bolan tucked the files under his arm and went into the room. The door closed behind him with a soft click. There were no windows. The only furniture in the office was a table and two chairs, one of them sprawled next to the door, as if Sparrow had kicked it away.

Bolan dragged the chair across the linoleum, causing the steel casters to squeal. Sparrow jerked in his chair, his handcuffs rattling. He'd been restrained further; a chain ran from his handcuffs to the ones around his ankles. He grimaced unhappily as he caught sight of Bolan. "You," he said.

"I'm getting tired of that," Bolan replied. "Cooper."

"What?"

"My name is Cooper. Yours is Sparrow. There. Now we're introduced." Bolan grabbed the table and shoved it aside, so that his chair was separated from Sparrow's by only a leg's length of empty floor. "I know who you are. I've read your file. Well, both files—Interpol sent over your European one an hour ago. And the FBI and BATF have a filing cabinet on the little commune you came out of." The Society of Thylea had kept a lower profile than most extremist groups, but they weren't as secret as they liked to claim. They had too many fingers in too many pies to avoid leaving substantial traces, and Kurtzman had begun tracking those leads back to their sources. Eventually, they would find the money men behind the whole operation, of that Bolan had no doubt. He was looking forward to it.

Sparrow's expression contorted. "You can't make me talk—*Vril-YA!*" The shout hung awkward and limp in the air before dissipating. Sparrow deflated into sullen silence.

"I don't intend to make you do anything," Bolan said. "I'm not you." He pulled the files out from under his arm and dropped them on the floor at Sparrow's feet. "I'm not going to torture you the way you tortured Agent Ogilvy. According to the Bureau, you and your pals kept him alive for four days. Or, rather, he held out for four days. They made them tough in Frank's day. I bet it took you two days to even get him to make a sound." Bolan spun his chair around and sat down, his elbows braced across the back. "No, Sparrow, I'm not going to lay a finger on you."

Sparrow smirked. That faded as Bolan continued, "If I were, I would start with your feet." He drew his knife and sent it hurtling down with such force that the blade sank into the floor. Sparrow blinked, swallowed and tried to shrink back into his chair. His eyes were drawn inexorably to the knife, as if it exerted a gravitational pull. It was one thing to face off against a man on even ground, but it was something else again to show bravado while handcuffed to a chair in a dim, bad-smelling back-room office. Bolan leaned over and tapped the pommel of the knife. "After your feet, I'd start on your shins. Then your thighs, and then your shoulders, arms and finally, hands." Bolan continued in that vein for several minutes, keeping his voice even and almost bored-sounding as he described the most grisly tortures his years of experience could conjure. The Executioner had been tortured more than once and he knew what he was talking about.

Sparrow's eyes got wider and wider, until they were fairly starting from his head. Oh, you must have been fun to play poker with, Bolan thought, watching the other man's face. Sparrow had no way of knowing that there was no man less likely to employ torture than the Executioner. Sometimes unpleasant methods were necessary to extract pertinent information, but this was not one of those situations, and Sparrow was not such a hard case. He was tough, but he was also running on fumes. Bolan was a good judge of character, and he had pegged Sparrow for a rapidly deflating balloon. He had the air of a man who was desperately trying to stay on his feet as the sand shifted beneath him.

Finally, Bolan said, "But I'm not going to do any of that to you, Sparrow. And do you know why?"

Sparrow's Adam's apple bobbed and he warbled, "W-why?"

Bolan leaned forward, tipping his chair. Sparrow flinched back, but Bolan's big hand shot out with the speed of a striking snake, and his fingers clamped across the back of the other man's head. With a gentle squeeze, he jerked Sparrow close. "Because you're going to tell me everything I want to know *right now*."

And he did. Words spilled out of Sparrow's mouth like a torrent. Bolan sat and took it all in, rarely interrupting, just listening. Then, when Sparrow was done, Bolan retrieved his knife, rose and left him sitting hunched over in his seat.

In the corridor, Bolan said, "I'm going to need transport. Sparrow said the others will be leaving as soon as they realize he's not going to show up. He said there's a bush pilot waiting for them at Merrill Field, in Anchorage."

"That makes sense. It's a general-use airfield," Ferguson said, nodding. "A lot of pilots out there make their living ferrying groups into the bush."

"Well, Sparrow's boss—Mervin—has apparently hired one. We're still in the layover window, but I reckon we have about four hours before they're in the wind." Bolan sheathed his knife. "It'll take three to get there."

"No time to scramble Lyons or the rest of Able Team for backup," Brognola said sourly. He met Bolan's gaze. "Guess you're still at bat, Striker."

"I wouldn't have it any other way," Bolan said, and he meant it. There were times when it was useful to be part of a team, but this wasn't one of them. One man could act with more speed than a group, even a group as effective as the Stony Man–based Able Team, and if there was ever a situation that required speed, this was it.

"We can roust a cargo flight and probably get you there in two, two and a half," Brognola said, thinking quickly. "Did he give you descriptions? Hell, did he tell you where they were planning to go?"

"Close enough," Bolan said. He looked at Ferguson. "I need to know exactly where HYPERBOREA is, just in case I can't catch them."

"How will you get out there?"

"Hopefully I won't have to," Bolan said. "If I do, I'll improvise. Can you make some calls?" he asked Brognola. "We need to give the Feds some warning, just in case it all goes to hell."

"I'll get on it. By the way, I brought your cold-weather gear, just in case," Brognola said. "It sounds like you're going to need it."

11

Merrill Field, Alaska, 3 hours later

Ida Blackjack leaned against the DHC-6 Twin Otter and gave Saul Mervin her best fish eye. The woman was slim, but not skinny, and of Inupiat heritage. She put Mervin in mind of the actress Irene Bedard. Black hair, cropped short, was hidden beneath a stained handkerchief, and smudges of oil and grease marred her features and jumpsuit. She methodically wiped her hands with a rag that was more dirt than cloth. "You said there'd be two more."

"Plans change," Mervin said.

"Huh."

Mervin cocked his head. "The pay will be the same."

"Damn right," Blackjack replied, flinging the rag across her shoulder. "You want me to take you into the middle of nowhere, I expect to be compensated." Her gaze slid past Mervin to where Kraft leaned against the hangar door, arms crossed. "Your pal doesn't talk much."

"He is my employee, and no, he does not," Mervin

said. He clasped his hands behind his back and tried not to let his irritation show. "Is this the plane?"

"Yep," Blackjack said. She knocked her knuckles against the metal frame. Mervin examined the aircraft, facts swimming across his mind. The Twin Otter was a Short Takeoff and Landing utility aircraft, with two engines and a passenger capacity of nineteen. It was a stereotypical bush plane, capable of breaching the far reaches of the Arctic, where other craft couldn't go. In short, it was exactly what was required to complete the task at hand.

It had taken the Society of Thylea years and money and blood to discover the existence of HYPERBOREA. They'd heard rumors, conspiracy theories— an American research base, clinging like a barnacle to the outer rim of the Arctic, the purpose and eventual fate of which was the subject of much speculation.

But Mervin, with his amazing brain, turned speculation to fact. Kraft had tracked down every living soul who had possessed even the slightest scrap of information regarding HYPERBOREA and its devilish secret. Finally, Mervin had assembled the pieces that had been so painstakingly gathered and the secret of HYPERBOREA was revealed.

To say that his masters, the Sun-Koh, had been impressed was treating it lightly. They'd been ecstatic. Those old men, gathered together in secret to plot and scheme, rattling on about Aryan purity and the lost empire of mighty Thylea, didn't have the wisdom to see what Mervin saw. To them, the secret of HYPERBOREA was another cog in their engine of delusion. But to Mervin it was a stepping stone to something better. And he was eager to begin.

"Get it ready. We will be leaving today," Mervin said.

"Short notice." Blackjack raised an eyebrow.

"It is a plane, not a space shuttle," Kraft said dismissively. It was the first time he had spoken in Blackjack's presence, and her eyes narrowed.

"You know anything about planes?" she asked.

"Quite a bit," Kraft said.

"Then why aren't you flying your pals out into the big white nothing?"

"Perhaps I should," Kraft said as he pushed away from the door.

Mervin raised a hand. "An arrangement has been made." He looked at Blackjack. "Double your fee, if you are ready within the hour."

"Triple."

"Double and a bonus to be determined upon return to Anchorage," Mervin countered. He could sense Kraft seething behind him, and he fought to restrain a smirk. Blackjack eyed him for a moment and then spit in her hand and extended it. Mervin hesitated, but only for an instant. Then he followed suit and shook Blackjack's hand. He was rewarded by a grin from her and an intake of outraged breath from Kraft.

"Your pal doesn't like me much," Blackjack said as she released his hand.

"He doesn't like anyone much."

Mervin and Kraft left the hangar and headed back toward the trio of SUVs that had brought them from the hotel. They'd checked out earlier in the day when Sparrow failed to call from Seattle. Boyd and the others piled up their gear on the tarmac in front of the hangar. None of them was armed, but their weapons were in easy reach, just in case.

"Employee, am I?" Kraft murmured. He sounded amused.

"Would you rather I had said that we were brothers in a nihilistic secret society, hell-bent on eradicating three-fourths of the human population, including her?" Mervin asked.

Kraft made a face. "I still think we should simply take the plane."

"Killing her would attract more attention than we need at this juncture," Mervin said. His mouth tasted of tar. He desperately wanted a cigarette. "Kill her as soon as we get where we're going, if you like."

"I was planning on it," Kraft said. He sounded pleased at the prospect. Mervin had never understood the appeal of casual murder. Killing Kraft, on the other hand, an acquaintance of long association, would be a delight.

Sparrow's failure annoyed Mervin. It also caused him some apprehension, though he wasn't planning on admitting it to anyone. Was the same man interfering again? Sparrow had sworn that he'd killed him, but what if… Mervin tried to push the thought aside, but it crept back with stubborn persistence. The plane from Seattle had arrived on schedule, but neither Sparrow nor Ackroyd had been aboard. As soon as he was certain that something had gone wrong, Mervin had flipped mental gears to Plan "B."

The absence of Ackroyd was the greater loss of the two. Mervin had been planning to have Sparrow killed anyway, but Ackroyd was a necessary component of the plan. Ackroyd was the only man who knew how to get into HYPERBOREA. Without him, they would be forced to employ less-effective measures.

Boyd dropped a duffel bag on the tarmac and Mervin flinched. "Careful!" he snapped.

"The explosives will not go off from being jostled," Kraft said. A glare from the big man stifled the resultant chuckles, but Mervin frowned regardless.

He hated them so much. Idiots, brutes and thugs—they deserved what they had coming. He knew that they called him the Tick-Tock Man behind his back. He knew that they hated him as much as he hated them. Mervin was only tolerated because of his intelligence. *You think you're warriors, and maybe you are, you atavistic simpletons. But I am a warrior, as well,* he thought, with a flush of savage pleasure. With jittery fingers he reached for his pack of cigarettes. Kraft's hand snapped out, snatching it from him.

"No."

"Give that back," Mervin whined. He couldn't help it. He was nervous and angry and he hadn't had a cigarette in over an hour. The nicotine lash caressed him and he spat, "Give it to me!"

"No," Kraft said. "We are standing in front of an airplane hangar. Can't you smell the fuel fumes? There is a very good chance that one spark could set something off, so…better safe than sorry."

Mervin hunched forward with a grunt. He clenched his hands so tightly that his knuckles turned white and he gritted his teeth. "Fine," he snarled. "I'm going to go find a place where I *can* smoke." He snatched the pack out of Kraft's hand and stalked off.

He could feel Kraft's eyes following him the entire way. Mervin wanted nothing more than to pull the .22 holstered beneath his coat and put a round between Kraft's eyes with mathematical precision. He was quite a good shot, though Kraft didn't know that.

But he couldn't do it. Not yet. In fact, he didn't know exactly when he was going to do it, but their mysterious opponent had provided him with the perfect opportunity to hide his tracks. The disappearance of Mervin and his cohorts in the Arctic wilderness would be put down to enemy action. Mervin would be free to change his name and face and sell the thing they sought to the highest bidder.

He knew what it was. He knew the scientists had processed and extracted the plague they had dubbed "Ymir," and that there were likely samples remaining. Even if there weren't, he had all the equipment he needed to parcel out the contagion and provide each of them with an infectious dose. Then the group would split up—each man going to a different international airport—and from there, they would drive a biological dagger into the guts of the world.

At least…that had been the plan he'd concocted for the Sun-Koh. Those demented old men had fallen for it completely, as had Kraft and the others. They wanted nothing more than to sacrifice themselves for the glory of their cause. And Mervin fully intended to allow them to do so. But he would not be joining them.

No, he intended to sell Ymir to the highest bidder. The U.S. government alone would likely pay him an exorbitant amount to return their lost property. Or, if he were feeling entrepreneurial, he could dilute the samples and parcel them out to a variety of groups. He felt less enthusiastic about the latter—in the wrong hands, Ymir would be dangerous. Mervin didn't fancy becoming exceedingly wealthy only to die choking on his own boiling juices. He might simply sell a placebo, after a controlled demonstration.

Mervin stopped, a cigarette halfway to his lips, wondering if the research staff at HYPERBOREA had made recordings. If so, they would prove useful. New plans sprang from that thought, spreading like webs across the surface of his mind. He hummed to himself as he grabbed the cigarette between his lips and lit it. He looked out across Merrill Field. From where he was standing—behind the hangar Blackjack was using—Mervin could see the runway.

Puffing happily, he warmed himself with thoughts of what was to come. And he wondered if he ought to thank their opponent, whoever he was, for providing him with the opportunity to free himself from the shackles of the Society of Thylea.

"You shouldn't smoke. It's bad for your health."

Mervin froze. The cigarette tumbled from his lips and fell to the tarmac, where it smoldered. He felt something hard and cold and very, very sharp brush against his throat. It was a knife, and a large one, held by a large hand.

The voice, rough and calm, continued. "Are you armed?"

"Y-yes," Mervin whispered. He felt his bowels loosen, and he closed his eyes, fighting the urge to wet himself. Terror blossomed in sharp bursts, making it hard to think.

"Where is it?"

"Under my right arm," he said. He felt a hand reach into his coat, and his .22 was plucked from its holster.

"I've been watching you for the past twenty minutes. I know who you are and what you're planning…

FREE Merchandise is 'in the Cards' for you!

Dear Reader,

We're giving away FREE MERCHANDISE!

Seriously, we'd like to reward you for reading this novel by giving you **FREE MERCHANDISE** worth over $20. And no purchase is necessary!

You see the Jack of Hearts sticker above? Paste that sticker in the box on the Free Merchandise Voucher inside. Return the Voucher promptly...and we'll send you valuable Free Merchandise!

Thanks again for reading one of our novels—and enjoy your Free Merchandise with our compliments!

Pam Powers

Pam Powers

P.S. Look inside to see what Free Merchandise is **"in the cards"** for you!

W

e'd like to send you two free books like the one you are enjoying now. Your two books have a combined price of over $10, but they are yours to keep absolutely FREE! We'll even send you 2 wonderful surprise gifts. You can't lose!

The Amazon never shares its secrets without a price...

ROGUE Angel
Alex Archer
RIVER OF NIGHTMARES

Don Pendleton's
The Executioner
BREAKOUT

A secret syndicate profits by freeing ruthless criminals...

REMEMBER: Your Free Merchandise, consisting of **2 Free Books** and **2 Free Gifts**, is worth over $20.00! No purchase is necessary, so please send for your Free Merchandise today.

Get TWO FREE GIFTS!
We'll also send you two wonderful FREE GIFTS (worth about $10), in addition to your 2 Free books!

Visit us at:
www.ReaderService.com

YOUR FREE MERCHANDISE INCLUDES...

2 FREE Books **AND** 2 FREE Mystery Gifts

Accepting your 2 free Action Adventure books and free gift (gift valued at approximately $5.00) places you under no obligation to buy anything. You may keep the books and gift and return the shipping statement marked "cancel". If you do not cancel, about a month later we'll send you 6 additional books and bill you just $31.94* - that's a savings of at least 24% off the cover price of all 6 books! And there's no extra charge for shipping and handling! You may cancel at any time, but if you choose to continue, every other month we'll send you 6 more books, which you may either purchase at the discount price or return to us and cancel your subscription. *Terms and prices subject to change without notice. Prices do not include applicable taxes. Sales tax applicable in N.Y. Canadian residents will be charged applicable taxes. Offer not valid in Quebec. Books received may not be as shown. All orders subject to credit approval. Credit or debit balances in a customer's account(s) may be offset by any other outstanding balance owed by or to the customer. Please allow 4 to 6 weeks for delivery. Offer available while quantities last.

If offer card is missing write to: Harlequin Reader Service, P.O. Box 1867, Buffalo, NY 14240-1867 or visit www.ReaderService.com ▲

BUSINESS REPLY MAIL

FIRST-CLASS MAIL   PERMIT NO. 717   BUFFALO, NY

POSTAGE WILL BE PAID BY ADDRESSEE

HARLEQUIN READER SERVICE

PO BOX 1867

BUFFALO NY 14240-9952

NO POSTAGE
NECESSARY
IF MAILED
IN THE
UNITED STATES

you and the eleven men you're with. You are going to come with me and I am going to restrain you. If you try to fight me, or if you call for help, I'll kill you. Do you understand?"

"Y-yes," Mervin mumbled. He didn't think the man was bluffing.

"Good. Start walking," the voice said. The knife was pulled away from his flesh. Mervin began walking. His mind reeled. What was going on? He needed a cigarette. His hands twitched. He needed a minute to think. Just a minute…

"Mervin, where are you going?" Kraft called out.

Mervin turned and saw Kraft approaching, one hand reaching beneath his coat, his eyes widening. He saw his captor for the first time—a tall man, rangy but muscular, with hard features and icy blue eyes that flashed first to Kraft and then to him. The blue-eyed man recognized him, he could see it! Mervin screamed and hurled himself to the side, out of the reach of that terrible knife the man still held loosely in one big fist.

"Kill him, Kraft! Kill him!"

12

The Executioner moved with lightning speed, covering the distance between himself and the man called Kraft in an eye-blink. Bolan still held the combat knife clutched in one hand and as he closed in, he swept the blade out in a vicious slash. It tore through the sleeve of the other man's coat and Kraft staggered, forgetting about the pistol Bolan knew he'd been reaching for.

Kraft hissed and backed away, blue eyes narrowing. Bolan fell into a knife-fighting stance, the combat knife held low and extended, as he examined his opponent. They were of a size, both big men, but Kraft had more muscle packed onto his frame. They circled one another slowly. Bolan made sure to keep the thin man in sight, as well. If he was the man Sparrow had mentioned—Mervin—Bolan had no intention of letting him escape.

"Who are you?" Kraft asked, examining the blood on his palm.

Bolan didn't reply. He could tell from the way the big man moved that he was dangerous. There was a lethal poetry to him that the Executioner recognized. His Heckler & Koch UMP .45 was strapped across his back, and the Desert Eagle was on his hip, but he knew with certainty that if he made a motion toward either, Kraft would be on him.

"Cat got your tongue?" Kraft asked, wiping his hand on his coat. "Good knife, there. I've got one myself." He reached behind him with his other hand still extended to counter any thrust Bolan might make, and drew a straight-edged knife from a sheath on his belt. "It's a *Nahkampfmesser,* a trench knife. My great-grandfather carried it in the First World War. It has shed much blood, this blade. Yours has, too, I'd wager," Kraft continued congenially.

"Stop talking and kill him, Kraft!" Mervin yelped, pressing himself flat against the side of the hangar.

"I do not tell you how to make your little plans, Mervin. Kindly do not tell me how to kill a man," Kraft said, his tone chiding. He met Bolan's cold gaze and shrugged. "It is hard to work with people who do not understand, eh? I know you know what I'm talking about. You've got the look, same as me."

"I'm nothing like you," Bolan said.

"He speaks!" Kraft said. "For a moment, I feared you were a mute. It is only a guess, but I'd say you are the reason Sparrow could not join us. Am I right?"

Bolan lunged. The KA-BAR combat knife slashed out and Kraft caught his wrist. Bolan grunted as Kraft's fingers tightened and a spasm of pain thrummed through his tendons. The trench knife dug for his face and Bolan grabbed Kraft's hand. The tableau held for a moment. The only sound was the occasional quiet grunt of effort from one of the combatants. Then the stalemate was broken in a flurry of motion as Bolan hooked Kraft's ankle with his own and the latter's knee drove upward, seeking Bolan's groin.

Both men fell only to leap to their feet moments later like contesting lions. Kraft's blade hissed out and parted the flesh of Bolan's cheek, releasing a spray of red into the cold Alaskan air. The Executioner gave no sound of pain, and his own blade drew a toll from Kraft's neck. Kraft cursed and reeled, launching an awkward kick that caught Bolan full in the chest and drove him back into the side of the hangar. The combat knife was knocked from the Executioner's grip, and the UMP dug painfully into his back.

Kraft dove upon him with a hoarse cry of triumph. Bolan caught his wrist, halting the tip of the trench knife mere inches from his eye. They strained against one another for a moment, Kraft pressing down with all of his weight, and Bolan resisting with every ounce of muscle he possessed.

Bolan jerked Kraft's arm to the side before bringing the man's wrist down on his upraised knee. Kraft's fingers opened and the knife fell. Quickly, Bolan flung up an elbow and caught his opponent in the face. Kraft staggered, disoriented. Bolan lunged forward, tackling him. Kraft's hands snapped up and his palms crashed against Bolan's ears. The Executioner rolled away, clutching his head, and Kraft followed him, one big fist thundering down to catch Bolan across the jaw.

They rolled across the ground, struggling. Bolan's fingers sought Kraft's eyes, and the big man gave a yowl as they connected. He reared to his feet and stumbled back, momentarily blinded. Bolan twisted and kicked out, knocking Kraft to the ground.

The Executioner rose and took the opportunity to

drag the UMP around, taking aim at the big man.
Kraft climbed onto his haunches and scraped blood
from his face. Bolan's punch had busted his nose, but
Kraft didn't seem to mind. He smiled widely. "Good,"
he wheezed. "Good fighter. Sparrow was right to be
worried about him, eh, Mervin?"

Bolan had lost track of the thin man during the
scuffle. He glanced to the side and saw Mervin raise
his reclaimed .22 in one shaking hand. The pistol
spoke and Bolan threw himself to the side. His UMP
spat in reply, the noise suppressor choking its growl
to a muted grumble. Mervin hurled himself to the
ground as Bolan's shots punched through the side of
the hangar.

Kraft sprang to his feet, scooped up his blade and
dove at Bolan with a berserk cry. Bolan, on one knee,
blocked the blow with his gun, but he was carried
backward by the force of Kraft's charge. The moment
his back touched the ground, Bolan drove his knees
up, striking Kraft in the belly and sending him flying.
Before he could do more than get to his feet, however,
Mervin was screaming for help.

An AR-15 opened up in reply, chewing the ground
between the two hangars. Bolan scrambled for cover
as Kraft hauled Mervin to his feet and went the other
way.

Bolan barreled through the hangar's side door just
in time to see the twin-engine DHC-6 roll onto the
tarmac, engines buzzing. The doors were open and
men in gray winter gear were throwing heavy duffel
bags inside. Two of them saw Bolan and raised their
weapons. Bolan ducked out of sight behind an indus-
trial air compressor as the gunmen fired.

Bullets rattled off the compressor and punched holes in several fuel drums nearby. A strong smell filled the hangar, reminding Bolan of the warehouse. He knew a rogue spark could easily lead to a repeat of that earlier conflagration.

Bolan heard a shout and, peering carefully around the compressor, he saw a slim shape drop out of the plane and race toward the gunman. The Executioner winced as the woman slammed a wrench across the back of a gunman's head. The man fell onto his hands and knees and another turned, surprised. The wrench snapped out again, catching him in the face, and the second man dropped his gun as he cried out.

Bolan seized the moment, rising from cover and firing from the hip as he raced forward. The gunman with the busted face spun about with a strangled cry and crumpled to the tarmac. The other scrambled away as his companions caught on to what was happening. The woman stared at Bolan in apparent shock and said something, though he couldn't make it out over the noise of the plane. She made as if to raise the wrench, when Kraft grabbed her from behind, one arm wrapping around her neck and the other extending over her shoulder, a 9 mm pistol in his hand. The pistol barked and Bolan jumped back as it struck the tarmac. He half raised the UMP but couldn't fire for fear of hitting the woman.

"That's far enough, my friend," Kraft called out. "Yes, that is quite far enough. It seems our pilot has decided to throw in her lot with you. Very disappointing, but unsurprising, given her savage nature."

"Savage *what?*" the woman shouted. "I was just

trying to keep these assholes from blowing up my hangar! I *paid* for that hangar!"

"Be that as it may, I now have no choice but to kill you. It will give me no small pleasure, you understand, but it is nonetheless inconvenient." Kraft smiled thinly and locked eyes with Bolan. The Executioner caught sight of Mervin sliding into the cockpit, his face pinched and tense. "But first, I must say *auf wiedersehen* to you, my friend. It was a fine dance, albeit brief, but it is over."

"Hell with that," the woman snarled. Her head snapped back, further squashing Kraft's already pulverized nose. The big man stepped back with a yelp, shaking his head. Bolan stretched out a hand and she took it without hesitation. With a jerk of his arm, Bolan whipped her behind him even as he caressed the UMP's trigger.

Kraft scrambled for the plane as the last of his men still on the tarmac fell, his chest and face splashed with red. The men on the plane returned fire through the still-open doors, and Bolan ran for the dubious safety of the hangar, shoving the woman ahead of him as AR-15s tore the tarmac at his heels.

"What the hell is going on?" the woman yelled as they sought cover behind the air compressor that Bolan had abandoned only moments before. "Who are you? Why are you shooting up my hangar?"

"Cooper, Justice Department," Bolan snapped, yanking her down. "Keep your head down, damn it!"

"Justice…? *Shit*," she hissed. "I knew it. I knew they weren't from the goddamn Department of Natural Resources. One of 'em is German, for God's sake." She tapped the air compressor with her wrench. "Stupid!" More bullets ripped through the hangar. "Stop shooting up my hangar, you bastards! It's full of fuel!" she shouted.

"I think that's the idea," Bolan said. He peered over the top of the compressor and saw that Kraft had climbed into the cockpit, shoving Mervin aside. His men were pulling the doors shut as the plane began to roll toward the runway.

"They're taking my plane," the woman said. "My goddamn plane!"

"Maybe not." Bolan sprang out from behind the compressor, UMP rising as he headed for the hangar doors. There was a chance he could disable one of the engines and prevent the plane from taking off. But even as he raised his submachine gun, Kraft kicked open the cockpit door and swung half out, a flare gun in one hand. He grinned wildly and bellowed, "To Valhalla with you!"

Kraft fired, and the flare streaked into the hangar. The woman shot past Bolan, running in the obvious direction. The Executioner, knowing what was coming, followed suit, and just in the nick of time.

The hangar exploded a moment later, and the world was filled with fire.

13

"They took my plane," the woman said, coughing, as Bolan helped her to her feet.

"I noticed. They also blew up your hangar." Bolan looked at the flames and then back at her. She was quite attractive, he noted. For a moment another face, with a similar sort of toughness, superimposed itself over hers and Bolan shook his head, dismissing the thought.

"I'm going to kill them," she snarled.

"No, I am," Bolan said, more harshly than he'd intended. The plane had taken off. It was hurtling northwest as fast as its engines could carry it. Thanks to Ferguson, however, he knew where it was headed. There was an old trading post near HYPERBOREA, abandoned since the beginning of the twentieth century. The government had used it as a layover point, to drop off supplies and pick up passengers from the research base, which was reachable only by hiking or by boat. A quick, terse inquiry and he got confirmation from the woman.

"Yeah, that's where they were going, all right. I thought they were heading into the Noatak Preserve for some hunting, the way they were talking. There are plenty of old fur-trade setups out there and a lot of campers use them as way stations." She looked at him. "It's Blackjack, by the by."

"What?"

"My name," she said, wiping dirt off her trousers. "Ida Blackjack."

"Mine's—"

"Cooper, yeah, you said. What are they—terrorists?"

"Something like that," Bolan replied. "They've got some unpleasant plans, and I need to stop them."

"A plane is what you need," Blackjack said, looking across the airfield.

"That would be helpful," Bolan agreed. There was no give in Blackjack. She was tough and adaptable, as well as quick thinking. Bolan admired those qualities.

"You need a pilot, too," she continued.

"I'm capable of flying a plane," Bolan said.

Blackjack gave him a look. "Hey, me, too, but they stole my plane. I want it back. If you're going after them, I'm going with you."

Bolan hesitated but not for long. He didn't have time to argue. "Fine, but I'm in charge."

"Yes, sir," Blackjack said, saluting casually. "Hot damn, let's go commandeer us a plane, huh, Cooper?" She clapped her hands together and strode off determinedly, leaving the warehouse burning merrily behind them. Bolan followed her more slowly. Men and women were hurrying toward the warehouse and shouting questions. He could hear fire engines and the more strident whine of police sirens. Merrill Field was about to be swarming with various elements of local authority.

Bolan paused only to retrieve his cold-weather

gear, including a heavy coat and a more durable version of his satellite phone, insulated against low temperatures. They weren't heading into the Arctic as such, but they'd be close enough. Bolan had operated in a variety of low-temperature theaters throughout his war, and he knew better than to leave such things to chance.

"There we go. That's Old Man Fortier's plane. He still owes me from that poker game last month. Plus, I know he keeps the fuel tanks topped up, just in case he gets a drop-in booking." They picked up the pace, heading for a brightly painted Maule M-7-235. Blackjack ducked under a wing and reached beneath a strut. "He always keeps a spare key down here. Get in," she said.

Bolan did. A fire engine raced past, sirens blaring. "Why are you coming with me?" he asked as she began flicking switches. "Really, I mean."

"The way I see it, I owe you a flight. You saved me back there," Blackjack said. "Plus, like I said, they took my plane. I want it back. You have a problem with that?"

"If I did, you wouldn't be here," Bolan said, strapping in.

"So who are they? They didn't look like any sort of al Qaeda agents to me."

"Terrorists come in all shapes and sizes," Bolan said.

They taxied onto the runway. A voice squawked querulously on the radio, and Blackjack switched it off. She leaned forward, peering up at the sky as the Maule rolled forward, engine rumbling. "I think we're clear."

"You think?"

"Pretty sure," Blackjack said. The Maule didn't require as long a runway as some of the larger planes, and they bumped into the air relatively swiftly. Bolan leaned back in his seat as the single-engine plane climbed to its flying altitude. He fished a first-aid kit out from under his seat and began to patch the cut on his cheek. It wasn't deep, but it would likely leave a scar. Another one for the collection, he thought with grim amusement.

Despite having a chance to rest on the flight from Seattle, a bone-deep ache still afflicted him. He'd pushed his body close to its limits, and it was informing him in no uncertain terms that he was fast approaching the wall. He pressed himself farther back in his seat and tried to relax.

Eyes closed, Bolan called to mind the map of Alaska he'd memorized before leaving Seattle. The Executioner had trained his mind to operate with an organizational clarity second to none. He knew that the Noatak Preserve had been established in 1978 to protect the area around the Noatak River Basin, above the Arctic Circle. HYPERBOREA was just north of that, somewhere close to the Chukchi Sea. If his enemies followed the Noatak River 70 or 80 miles upstream, they would run right into the base. It would mean several days of hard travel, but the Preserve often played host to sport hunters. A group of armed men wouldn't attract much notice.

He felt a certain grudging admiration for Saul Mervin—from what Kurtzman had been able to scrounge up, the so-called Tick-Tock Man was a first-class criminal mind. Mervin had crafted more than a dozen schemes for the Society of Thylea.

The man's current plan was like clockwork, in its way, clicking along with a ruthless, mechanical surety. There were a dozen separate elements at work, and the timing had been all-important. If Ferguson hadn't brought Brognola in, and if Bolan hadn't been in Reno at the right time, they would never have caught up to the bad guys before Ackroyd was taken to Alaska. As it was, he was still a step or two behind. His only real advantage was that they had no idea who he was or what sort of resources he could bring to bear. At the same time, thanks to Sparrow, Bolan knew enough about them to tailor his plans appropriately.

From Ferguson, he knew that Ackroyd was the sole remaining individual who knew the code to open HYPERBOREA—likely the reason the Society wanted him. He was also the only man alive who knew anything about Ymir. From Sparrow, Bolan knew that Ackroyd's absence wasn't a deal breaker. They'd just as happily blow the doors down and risk damaging the very thing they sought. They weren't stupid, but they were fairly single-minded. They'd slug their way through any obstacles and take the quickest, most direct route to their destination. Which meant…what? Traveling overland would take them far too long, especially now. So that left the river.

His eyelids cracked open. "This trading post you were dropping them off at, have you ever been there before?"

"Only to pass over it on the way to Wainwright or Noatak," she said. "It'll take us about three hours, depending on the weather. They've got a half hour lead, but we're lighter, so we might be able to catch up, if that's what you're worried about. Even if we don't, we won't lose them."

"I'm not worried about that." He frowned. "How much equipment did they have?"

"A good bit," Blackjack said.

"Did any of it resemble an inflatable motorboat?" Bolan asked. "They might have had the motor itself broken down into its component parts."

"Could have been," she said doubtfully. "You think they're planning to go upriver?"

"I'm counting on it," Bolan said. "They'll be moving quickly, and even traveling upriver, against the current, they'll move faster than trying to hoof it." He shrugged. "It's what I would do, at any rate."

"And you think like them, huh?"

"Close enough," Bolan said.

"You're an odd guy, Cooper," Blackjack said.

"So I've been told." Bolan leaned his head against the door and looked down as the natural beauty of Alaska passed beneath him.

"I didn't know they were terrorists," she said, after a few minutes of silence.

Bolan looked at her. "Did I say you did?"

"I just wanted to make a point of it. For the record," she said. Her tone was defensive. "I don't want you sending my ass to a federal pen or something. I want it clear that I wasn't aiding and abetting or nothing like that."

"I'll make a note of it in my report," Bolan said, fighting back a smile.

"You do that. Also, you think I'll get reimbursed for my hangar? Since I'm helping you and all?"

"Don't push your luck."

She fell silent. After a moment, she said, "What I can't figure is, why not just head up to Noatak and then go downriver? It'd be quicker."

Bolan had wondered this himself. "It might be quicker, but the likelihood of interference is higher. Everything I've seen so far implies that these men are prioritizing speed and a lack of interference over everything else. Frankly, if they hadn't tried to kidnap a man, no one would have been able to stop them. No one would have had time. When one strategy failed, they immediately implemented a second. If the weather had been bad, or I had been delayed in some way, I wouldn't have caught up to you in time."

"And my hangar wouldn't have been blown up."

"And you would be dead," Bolan said. She didn't meet his gaze. She was a tough one, but even the toughest hesitated to contemplate her own demise. "They would have killed you, not because they bore you any grudge, but because that's what they do. If it's expendable, they get rid of it. It doesn't matter whether it's a building or a person—they'll even sacrifice their own people." He turned away. "Still glad you came?"

"Man, you know how much a plane costs? That thing is all I got. Flying is all I got. I slept in that damn hangar, I ate at the airport canteen, I got drunk at the airfield bar and I flew. If I don't get that plane back, I might as well not even exist." The words were heavy with feeling. Blackjack was a woman who lived close to the surface, and Bolan felt a subliminal tug as he looked at her strong features and dark eyes.

"If we don't stop them, that'll go for a lot more people than just you," Bolan said.

"I still don't get it. What the hell is up here? It's a damn nature preserve!"

Bolan said nothing. It wasn't his secret to share. And in truth, the fewer people who knew about Ymir, the better. The Society of Thylea wasn't the only group of psychopaths around for whom a prehistoric disease would make the perfect party favor.

While he hadn't cleared it with Brognola, the Executioner fully intended to end the threat posed by HYPERBOREA and the deadly secrets contained within. The pestilential threat that Ackroyd had described was just too monstrous to sit unprotected. If one group of madmen had found it, others could, as well.

One way or another, the Executioner wouldn't let that happen.

14

The DHC-6 landed with a soft bump. Kraft guided the bush plane to a stop and leaned back in his seat. Despite his distaste for the mud woman, he had to admit that she'd taken care of her craft. The three-hour flight had been as smooth as butter.

Although Kraft knew how to fly most types of planes, his experience with smaller aircraft was limited. That was one of the reasons they had hired a pilot in the first place—better to be safe than sorry.

Kraft looked out through the plane's windshield. The trading post was a ghost town, its three structures withered by the elements and close to a century's lack of upkeep. The single street had been widened and flattened several decades previously by the United States government, and now it served as a makeshift landing strip. There was also a station where a plane could be rolled beneath a tarp and protected from both the weather and airborne spies.

The paranoia of the American government was exceeded only by that of their enemies. The Cold War had been a strange time for everyone. Mervin would have been right at home, he thought, not unkindly.

"It is a bit unprepossessing, I admit, but Mervin

says this is the place, so it is the place." Kraft unbuckled his safety belt and looked across at Mervin, who was huddled in his seat, whey-faced and tight-lipped, as he had been since Merrill Field. Their attacker had rattled him. "It is the place, yes?"

Mervin didn't answer. Instead, he tore off his safety harness and flung open the door. He tumbled out onto the ground and vomited noisily. Kraft sighed and climbed out of the plane. Muted laughter threaded among the others, but Kraft ignored it. He circled the plane and saw Mervin on his knees, trying to pry a cigarette from his pack with trembling hands. "I hate flying," he croaked.

"Yes. You do not travel well." Kraft examined the cuts he'd sustained in the fight with their attacker. The man had been a devil with a blade. Kraft had rather enjoyed their brief set-to.

Mervin stabbed the cigarette between his lips and scrounged for his lighter. "They're laughing at me."

"Yes. I'll discipline them shortly," Kraft said. He crossed his arms and leaned against the plane. "Do you still consider him irrelevant?"

"Who?"

"Don't play dumb," Kraft chided.

"No," Mervin said. He gave a triumphant grunt as he found his lighter and applied it to his cigarette.

Kraft grimaced. Sometimes Mervin's addiction made him wonder about the other man. Mervin had one of the most impressive minds Kraft had ever encountered, but his insistence on cramming chemicals into his system was as blindly stupid as anything Kraft had ever seen.

"No, most definitely not," Mervin continued. "He's

very determined, that one." He got to his feet and peered down the road. There were few trees this close to the Arctic, and the horizon was barren. He shivered and pulled his coat tighter about himself. "We're almost there. A few days' travel upriver and we'll be there."

"Yes," Kraft said. He pushed himself away from the plane and followed Mervin's gaze. *"Jotunheim,"* he murmured, looking about. In many ways, Alaska was the land of his dreams. A land of frosty wastes and cold forests, where beasts still roamed and the gods might still walk. It was one of the last, almost pristine wildernesses left on the planet, where a man might test himself against nature. His breath plumed in the frosty air, and for a moment, he thought he could see strange shapes in it. The gods were watching them, he knew.

"Don't you mean Thylea?" Mervin asked.

"One and the same," Kraft said. "You realize that he will follow us." Mervin looked at him and Kraft sighed. "Blackjack survived. She knew where we were going. I have no doubt she will share that information."

"It doesn't matter. We outnumber him."

"That didn't seem to bother him overmuch at the airfield."

"Then what would you suggest?" Mervin asked.

"We wait. And then we end his interference, once and for all." Kraft called out to Boyd and the latter brought him a heavy duffel bag. Kraft sank to his haunches and unzipped the bag. Carefully, he removed a weighty length of equipment. Mervin gaped.

"What the devil is that?"

"This is an FIM-92 Stinger. It fires a SAM, a portable surface-to-air missile." Kraft frowned slightly. "You did ask me to prepare for all eventualities, you'll recall."

Mervin stared at him. "How many weapons did you bring?"

"Enough." Then, more seriously, he said, "Your plans are brilliant things, Mervin, but they are fragile in their intricacy. Therefore, I have taken the liberty of creating backup plans, just in case." He ignored Mervin's insulted blustering and stood, the Stinger in his hands. "We will wait, and I will remove our nameless friend from the equation. Then we will continue, unimpeded."

"How do you even know he's coming? Or that he's coming by plane?" Mervin demanded, chewing on his cigarette. His normally pale features were flushed and Kraft reflected briefly on the stresses his charge was under. Mervin had insisted on accompanying them, despite his obvious distaste for fieldwork.

"How do I know that he's coming? Because, Mervin, that's what I would do. How do I know that he's coming by plane?" He smiled slightly. "He was at an airfield."

Mervin's glare was beautiful in the purity of its hate. It was his own fault, and Mervin knew it. He had refused to believe that one man could disrupt his machinations, and now he appeared foolish for that insistence. The men, who had never respected the Tick-Tock Man, had even less reason to do so now.

"Help the others get the plane under cover while Boyd and I wait for our pursuer," Kraft said, hefting the Stinger and heading for one of the structures.

Boyd followed Kraft, hauling the satchel that held the SAMs. The buildings weren't tall, but they were surprisingly sturdy for their age and state. Kraft climbed one with a swift simian grace and Boyd followed suit, albeit more slowly. "He doesn't look happy," Boyd said.

"Mervin is rarely happy," Kraft replied, preparing the Stinger. "This escapade is not going according to plan, and that gives him the twitches." He sighed. "Still, this will be good for him. He needs to learn that life and death cannot be so callously planned. There is a difference between men and cogs, and he would do well to remember that."

"How long do you think we'll have to wait?" Boyd asked a few minutes later.

"Not long," Kraft said. He jerked his chin at the clear gray sky. "I caught sight of them an hour back. They're pushing that little plane hard."

Boyd whistled. "That was quick," he said, peering at the approaching dot. He glanced at Kraft. "You didn't say anything…"

"What would have been the point?" Kraft shrugged and stood. The Stinger was a sturdy presence on his shoulder and he peered through the targeting sight. "As I said before, he is determined. As determined as we are. Which means he will waste no time in following us," he said. Kraft pulled his face away from the Stinger and sighed. "It seems a shame, however. To kill such a man like this is wasteful."

"You mean sensible," Boyd said.

"I mean what I say. I understand that you lack the heroic instinct, but do try and understand. Destiny, Boyd, holds us in its claws. There will be songs sung of this quest in the years to come. The great Aryan empires which will arise to take their rightful place as masters of this wounded globe shall tell our story to children, to teach them of the harsh heroism required of the sons and daughters of Thylea." Kraft looked at him sadly. "It is only meet that we clash with an enemy equal to our heroism. That man speeding toward us, he is just such an enemy. And it makes my soul cringe to deal with him thus."

"Hasn't stopped you before," Boyd said pointedly. Kraft looked at him. The lanky Canadian met his gaze blandly, as if he had made a simple statement rather than an accusation. Kraft grunted.

"You are wise, in your way," he said.

"I'm a goddamn philosopher, Kraft. Now blow them bastards out of the air so we can get on with this," Boyd said dismissively. He gestured at the dot. It had drawn close enough that they could make out the number on the plane and hear the engines.

Kraft looked at him for a moment longer. Then, with a grimace, he did as the other man suggested. The SAM shot from the Stinger's muzzle and tore through the air, splitting the distance with a mechanical wail. The plane bucked and skewed sideways as the SAM struck the rear portion of the craft and tore it asunder. Trailing smoke and fire, the aircraft tumbled out of the sky. Kraft watched it fall with a dour expression. Then he shoved the Stinger into Boyd's arms and climbed down from his perch.

"What was that? Is it him?" Mervin shouted, running toward them.

"It was," Kraft said. "Let's go."

15

"What was that? What the HELL was that?" Black-jack screamed as warning lights flashed on the instrument panel. The frigid wind clawed its way into the cockpit through the hole that had been newly ripped into the side of the plane.

Bolan twisted in his seat and cursed as he grabbed his gear. "Probably a surface-to-air missile," he said. "I guess they don't want us to follow them." He could tell it had only been a glancing hit. If the missile had struck them full-on, it would have ripped the small plane apart.

"You think?" Blackjack shouted, banging her fist on the instrument panel. "We're a stone duck, Cooper! Our engine is gone!"

"Can you guide us in?" Bolan asked. The plane was tumbling through the air and only his safety belt was keeping him in his seat. His stomach lurched as the plane corkscrewed downward. The taiga loomed, filling the windshield.

"I can try!"

"What about parachutes?"

"Fortier doesn't trust them," Blackjack said, fighting with the controls. "I can guide us in, no problem. No problem."

Bolan bit back a curse. There was no time to think, no way to fight the cruel clutch of gravity. It wasn't often that the Executioner was forced to rely on others, and he didn't like the feeling.

"We're going in!" Blackjack said. "Hold on to your butt!"

Bolan tensed. The impact, when it came, was thunderous. Bolan was jerked forward and back, tossed about by the force of their landing. His head connected with something hard and he heard the teeth-shuddering sound of trees snapping and splintering. The world spun crazily for a moment and then blackness engulfed the Executioner.

Bolan had no way to tell how much time had passed when a growl woke him from his hazy dreams of blood and death. He hadn't been unconscious, not quite. The growl came again. It was a low-frequency rumble that Bolan's ancient ancestors would have recognized, even if he had not. It wasn't mechanical. The body of the plane creaked as a great weight jostled it. He looked around blearily. He was upside down.

Something stung Bolan's eyes. He touched his head and winced. His gloved fingers came away stained with red. Instinctively, he jerked his knife from its sheath and cut the safety belt holding him in place. He thudded down, and the plane's frame creaked again. Bolan could hear a snuffling sound, and a large brown shape passed through his limited field of vision.

"Bear," Blackjack said. She, too, was hanging upside down in her seat, held tight by her safety belt. She looked woozy and several shallow cuts marred her angular features. "Smelled the blood," she added, her words slightly slurred, "Probably scared it when we crashed." Bolan looked her over quickly. Thankfully her injuries were, like his, superficial. Neither of them seemed to have a concussion or any broken bones. He turned, his eyes surveying the interior of the cockpit. He couldn't see his UMP anywhere. It was likely lost in the crash. He could smell the strong stink of fuel, however.

"Well, let's see if we can't convince him to go somewhere else," Bolan said, levering himself around so that his feet pressed against the door. Besides the bear-stink, the smell of spilling fuel was getting stronger. They needed to get away from the plane as quickly as possible. Blackjack reached for him, her eyes wide.

"That's a grizzly bear!" she said. "Are you crazy?"

"I'm well aware of what it is, and probably, yes." Bolan pulled his legs back for a kick. "I'm going to lead it away. As soon as it's clear, put some distance between yourself and the plane. Grab as much of our gear as you can, but be quick." That said, he put all of the force he could muster into the blow. The door, already weakened by the crash, burst off its hinges and rattled across the ground. He heard the bear give a startled grunt but didn't hesitate. Combat knife in hand, he slithered out and climbed to his feet.

The grizzly was resting half on top of the plane, its bulk balanced awkwardly. The bear's eyes met his and its jaw sagged as it leaned forward and gave a bellicose roar. Bolan didn't flinch. There were few dangerous animals of one sort or another that the Executioner hadn't encountered in his long war. Familiarity, however, did not breed contempt. While Bolan had few compunctions about killing a dangerous man, he rarely killed animals unless absolutely necessary. That said, if it came down to it, he wouldn't hesitate.

The grizzly was a stereotypical example of the species—*ursus arctos horribilis,* the North American Grizzly bear. It was a male, for which he was thankful. There were few things more dangerous on the planet than an enraged she-bear, especially where its cubs were involved. Bolan made a quick estimate…. The animal was close to eight hundred pounds of muscle and fat, the latter indicating that it was preparing to go into hibernation, which also explained why it was looking at him as if he were the tastiest salmon in the river. The bear rumbled as it hunched forward, letting all of its weight fall onto the plane. Abused metal popped and squealed. Bolan stepped back. He needed to get it away from the plane. The Desert Eagle might put it down, if he hit the bear somewhere vital, but if he missed, he could set off the fuel that was spilling from the plane's ruptured fuselage. He held his hand out to the side and turned the blood-daubed fingers toward the bear. The cold breeze would carry the scent right to the big animal's quivering nostrils.

"You still alive?" Blackjack called out from within the plane.

"Yes, and stop distracting the bear, please," Bolan snapped.

"Just checking," Blackjack replied, sounding unduly cheerful. Bolan wondered whether she did have a concussion, after all. She'd obviously managed to get herself out of her seat. He hoped she'd have the good sense to remain out of sight until he'd lured the bear away.

The grizzly moved off the plane like a slow-motion avalanche of fur and muscle. Copious amounts of drool clung to its jaws and its square head swung from side to side as it looked him over. Then, with a grunt, it reared up on its hind legs and pawed the air.

Bolan's guts turned to ice as he looked up at the titanic beast. The Desert Eagle on his hip wasn't as reassuring as it had been a few moments earlier, and the combat knife even less so. As slowly as possible, he drew the pistol and held it down by his side. The bear bobbed its head as it sniffed the air. Bolan wondered whether it could smell the fuel, and whether the stink was confusing it.

He really didn't want to shoot. There was no telling whether the first shot would drop it, and if it didn't, there was a good chance he wouldn't get a second shot.

Snow began to spiral down from the gray sky as man and bear faced each other. The bear dropped onto all fours and grumbled. Bolan slowly raised the pistol. The animal gave a querulous grunt and Bolan readied himself. If it came at him, there was no way he could outrun it, so he'd have to take the shot.

His eyes met those of the bear. If it wanted a piece of him, it was going to have to earn it. Then a rifle cracked and the bear gave a startled whine and lumbered past him, leaving Bolan to stare after it in disbelief.

Blackjack leaned across the shattered wing of the plane, a rifle in her hands. She rolled off the wing and trotted toward him. "You missed," he said.

"I didn't try to hit it. You were keeping it occupied

so I figured a scare would convince it to leave." Black-jack tossed him his gear. She was wearing a backpack and had a bone-handled hunting knife belted to her waist. "No call to kill a critter if we don't have to."

Bolan holstered his pistol and knife and slid into his gear. "Smart thinking, regardless," he said.

"Would you really have taken it on?" she asked, peering at him.

"If I'd had to, yes," Bolan said, meeting her gaze.

"You aren't very smart, are you?"

Bolan smiled and said, "Nope. Now, let's—hsst!" His smile was wiped from his face by the sound of feet crunching through the snow. He grabbed Blackjack and pushed her into the trees. Then, acting quickly, he grabbed a branch dislodged by the crash, and used it to obliterate their tracks. A moment later they were crouching behind a fallen tree.

"Bear tracks," someone called out in a muffled voice. Two men stepped into sight, AR-15s in their gloved hands, their fur-lined hoods up over their heads and their faces hidden by ski masks. Kraft had sent men to check on the crash site. Blackjack raised her rifle. Bolan caught the barrel and pushed it down. He shook his head. The sound of gunshots would travel quite far, and now that he knew his enemies were listening, he didn't want them hearing anything that would bring more men running. There was no telling how far they were from the rest of the Society gun-men, but if these men could lead them back…

"Blood, as well," the other said, sinking to his haunches with his rifle across his knees. He touched the red splatter on the snow with two fingers. "Though not much," he added.

"A bear might not leave much," the first one said doubtfully. He sounded nervous.

"What—it carried them off? Get real, bears don't do that," the second said dismissively.

"How do you know what bears do?"

"I watch television," the second replied.

Bolan shifted his weight and dug his hand into the hard-packed ground. He tore loose a fairly dense chunk of sod and hurled it overhand at the plane. It connected with a thump. The nervous one spun about and his assault rifle chattered, stitching the wreckage. The spilled fuel caught and the plane blew with a monstrous roar. Bolan caught Blackjack and shielded her as wreckage went flying, and burning debris scattered about the clearing. The two gunmen were knocked sprawling but scrambled quickly to their feet to stare in consternation at the burning wreckage.

"What the hell did you do that for?" the second man snarled.

"I thought it was the bear!"

"Idiot." The second man shoved his companion toward the trees. "Let's get out of here. Kraft will want to know that there aren't likely to be survivors."

As the two Society of Thylea gunmen moved off, Bolan rolled off Blackjack, who cursed quietly. "Harry is going to kill me," she said.

"It was for a good cause," Bolan replied, pushing himself to his feet. "Let's go."

"I don't understand why you didn't let me shoot them," she grumbled, following suit. "I thought that was the whole reason we came out here."

"No, that's why I came out here. You invited yourself along," Bolan said. "And we need them to lead us to where we need to go. Unless you've got a GPS handy."

"No, but I do have a map," she countered.

"Good. See any reference points? Do you remember any from before we crashed?" Bolan asked calmly. She glared at him. He kept his expression serene. "No? Me, neither. I guess we follow them."

"I still don't see why you had to blow up the plane."

"I didn't want them sticking around to search for us. Between the bear tracks and the explosion, they'll assume we're dead. Which is the best advantage we could hope for at the moment, given that we're severely outgunned and outnumbered."

"If we're that bad off, why are you smiling?"

"Because," the Executioner said. "I've got them right where I want them."

16

Some hours later, Bolan crouched in the darkness, watching the flickering light of the campfire dance through the trees. They had reached the river after a hard day's hike, and now Kraft and the others had apparently made camp for the night. Bolan and Blackjack had followed at a distance, keeping well out of sight behind the cover of brush and rock. Blackjack had proved to have a sound knowledge of woodcraft, moving almost as quietly and quickly as the Executioner, though without his surety. She now hugged the rifle she'd salvaged from the plane as she lay on the cold ground, watching the flames alongside Bolan.

"How are we playing this?" she murmured softly as she blew into her hands. It wasn't quite winter yet, but it was plenty cold. Bolan could hear the burble of the Noatak nearby.

"We're not. I am," Bolan said. Carefully, he stripped off his coat and gear. The cold had its claws in him instantly, but he took several deep breaths, and felt his blood begin to circulate. The adrenaline would keep him warm, he knew. "You stay here."

"That's it?"

"No," Bolan said. He tapped the rifle's scope. "How good are you with one of these?"

"I wouldn't have taken it if I didn't know how to use it," she muttered, sounding offended. Fortier, the owner of the crashed plane, might not have believed in parachutes, but he did believe in self-defense. The rifle was a Winchester Model 70, a sporting rifle loaded with .458 Magnum cartridges, fully capable of bringing down big game animals. Fortier had apparently shot at least one bear, according to Blackjack. She had a box of cartridges in her coat pocket and a yen to use them, though Bolan suspected she was more than comfortable employing the buck knife on her belt in a life-or-death situation.

"Then cover me," he said. With that, he began to move toward the light of the fire. There would be sentries. Probably at least three, spaced at regular intervals.

Slowly, Bolan crept through the scrub, at one with the darkness. He'd rubbed dirt onto his features and onto the blade of his combat knife. He slid between the trees with a silent grace that a wolf would have envied. The first sentry was standing about twelve yards from the clearing where the group had made camp. His forearms were braced against the length of his rifle, which was slung across his body. He wasn't paying attention to anything in particular.

Careless, Bolan thought. They had little reason to be wary, but the sentry displayed a certain laxity that Bolan wouldn't have tolerated in his own men. Bolan slid around the sentry, moving between him and the light of the fire. The man noticed when the light dimmed and he turned. Bolan struck swiftly, grabbing his mouth and jaw in one hand and yanking his head back as he drove the KA-BAR combat knife up through his back and into his lungs. With a short, brutal twist of the blade, he pierced the man's heart a moment later. Then, holding tight to the trembling body, he lowered it to the ground, taking care to retrieve the sentry's weapon.

In the dim light, he checked the AR-15. A snapping twig alerted him to the approach of another gunman. "Hess? You got a smoke?" the sentry murmured. "Hess?"

Bolan acted quickly. With a speed and skill that had to be witnessed to be believed, he flung the knife point-first into the sentry's throat, knocking him backward. The man crashed down, and Bolan was on him a moment later, ripping the knife free and finishing the job. Bolan heard raised voices from the direction of the fire and rose into a half crouch. As the men began to call out to their dead companions, Bolan dropped to his belly and slithered through the tangled scrub. The gunmen began to spread out, and several had their weapons raised. Bolan took aim at them first. He stroked the trigger and the AR-15 sprayed the clearing. A man flopped backward, his own weapon going off as his fingers jerked convulsively on the trigger. Bolan made a quick battlefield calculation—three down, seven left. Still enough to be a problem, but a smaller problem than before, Bolan thought.

Bolan was up and moving, sprinting to another position. As he ran, he fired blind. There was little chance of him killing more than one or two of them, but that wasn't his intention. The rifle clicked and he tossed it aside as he threw himself into the underbrush. The remaining men were firing at random, spraying the trees with as much ammunition and as many curses as they could muster. Bark and torn branches fell atop Bolan, but he didn't move. One hand slipped to the Desert Eagle, but he didn't draw it. No sense wasting the ammunition. Not yet.

"Stop," Kraft roared. "Stop!" The big man had reared up in a way that was reminiscent of the bear and he flung out a hand, knocking one of his men down. "Fools," he bellowed. "He's making you waste ammunition. Stop firing!"

"Where is he? Where is he?" Mervin whined. The thin man had his little pistol in his hand and he was looking around wildly. "You said he was dead! Kraft, you said he was dead!"

"I was wrong," Kraft said, looking around. "It happens."

If Kraft hadn't been a racist, murdering psychopath, Bolan might have respected him for that admission alone. He'd met a number of men like Kraft in his long career. They possessed the talent for command but rarely had the self-awareness to know that talent didn't make them infallible. It was a dangerous combination. Bolan considered shooting him then and there, but he knew that the risk outweighed the potential gain.

"Up. Everyone up," Kraft said briskly, scanning the dark trees. "Gather your gear. Take only what you can carry. We're making a run for the boats." He looked at the trees. "Are you out there, my friend? Can you hear me? I assume so," he called out. "I assume you are watching us even now. Good. I am happy you are alive, my friend, though you may not believe me.

There are three motorized rafts set up on the shore. We are only taking two. You should feel free to use the last. If you live through the next few minutes, that is. Heinrich, Adams, keep his head down. The rest of you, go!"

Two of the remaining gunmen began to fire. Bolan pressed himself against the cold ground as they swept the area. Kraft hauled Mervin to his feet and they charged at the river with the others, firing as they went, weaving a wall of brass and lead to keep their unseen enemy at bay. As he hunkered down, Bolan hoped Blackjack had the good sense to keep her head down.

Soon, Heinrich and Adams slowly backed out of the clearing, firing intermittently as they retreated. Bolan watched them go but didn't move until he heard the growl of motors. Then he waited a ten count, pushed himself to his feet and stepped toward the still-crackling fire.

"Cooper?" Blackjack called.

"I'm here. Are you all right?" Bolan asked as she clambered into the open. She made a show of checking herself and nodded.

"Unperforated and unimpressed. You barely killed any of them." Blackjack looked around, frowning.

"I wasn't particularly trying to," Bolan countered, a bit taken aback. "As you so helpfully pointed out, we're outnumbered and outgunned, Ms. Blackjack. Right now, I'm just trying to even the odds." He looked in the direction Kraft and the others had fled. "We'll have to hope Kraft wasn't lying about the raft. Otherwise, it's going to be a long hike."

"We could just go back for my plane."

"Feel free," Bolan said. "I'm heading upriver."

"Not without me, you ain't!" Blackjack shot back quickly.

She glared at him and he gestured to the sputtering fire and the duffel bags their enemies had left behind. "Grab what you can easily carry. Ammunition and fuel take precedence, food is second. I'll see if there's really another raft." He met her still-simmering glare and said, "Look, many hands make quick work. If you want to help, help. If you want to argue, go back to your plane and wait."

Bolan moved quickly in the direction of the river. Blackjack was capable, but contentious and contrary to a fault. She wasn't used to being told what to do, and it showed. Bolan wondered whether he'd made a mistake in allowing her to come along.

The Noatak greeted him as he stepped down the slope and out of the trees. The sky was alive with stars, and the river looked like a ribbon of lit glass beneath their gaze. He heard the howl of a gray wolf and for a moment, the weight of his undertaking was lifted from his shoulders. The Executioner sucked in a lungful of clean air, tasting the forest and the river in one breath.

In the distance, cutting the horizon, was a line of mountains—the Schwatka Mountains. They were part of the Brooks Range, stretching from Alaska through to the Yukon. They seemed to bow with an immensity of age that struck a chord in Bolan. He shook his head, his breath pluming about his head like a halo. The cold wrapped around him and he repressed a shiver. He looked at the shore.

An inflatable raft with an attached motor had been left behind. Bolan quickly checked it over for booby traps, badly patched holes or anything that might have made the raft a trap rather than a strange gift. Finding nothing, he sat back on his heels, slightly puzzled. It was rare that he came across a man with a death wish as peculiar as Kraft's. To willingly provide Bolan with the means of catching up was unique. The Executioner had faced men who wanted to test themselves against him; that desire rarely lasted more than one encounter. In Kraft's case, it seemed to be growing stronger.

"Yeah, puzzling, ain't it?" a voice said. "Kraft's got a lot of bad habits—but being sneaky isn't one of them." Rocks shifted beneath a foot. "Luckily, he ain't in charge."

The soft hiss of metal and plastic cutting the air alerted Bolan to the man's intent a half second before the butt of the rifle caught him on the side of the head. Bolan staggered, off-balance and wide open as the length of the rifle caught him in the belly. The Executioner coughed and stumbled to the side. A knee caught him on the chin and then he was sliding through the wet stones, on his hands and knees, the world spinning out of control.

"You really thought you were going to take that damn raft and sail upriver after us, didn't you?" his attacker said, circling. A rough blow sent Bolan sprawling. A hand jerked his Desert Eagle out of its holster and tossed it aside. His attacker backed away and sat down on the edge of the raft. "You're either stupid or confident. Maybe a bit of both," he said.

Bolan, on his hands and knees, shook his head to clear it. His stomach rebelled at the movement and his head ached. He spat blood. "More one than the other," he said.

"Ha! You know, just because Kraft meant that 'honorable combat' bullshit don't mean it goes for everybody," the man said, raising his weapon. "The Tick-Tock Man might be a weird little bastard, but he is smart. He said to me, 'Boyd, Kraft will be upset, but he'll get over it' and you know what, damned if he isn't right."

Bolan tensed, readying himself to move. The Desert Eagle might as well have been miles away, but one good leap and he could grab it. He might take a bullet, but he would send one back if he could. Boyd smirked and sighted down the barrel. "Bye-bye, buddy," he said, as his finger tightened on the trigger.

The rifle cracked.

Boyd was knocked over backward, into the raft. He sprawled out in it, and his leg gave a twitch. His face had an expression of shock stamped on it. Bolan looked up and saw Blackjack work the bolt on her rifle. "He dead?" she called out.

Bolan looked at the entry wound in the man's chest and said, "He's dead."

"Told you I could shoot, Mr. Justice Department."

"See if he's the one with the keys to my plane. Ain't none of them other ones you killed got 'em."

"You shot him, you search him," Bolan said.

"That your way of saying thank you?"

"Thank you."

"You're welcome," Blackjack said primly.

17

Two days later

Mervin huddled behind a rock and stewed silently in his own growing anger. They were running low on fuel and food. There was plenty of the latter in the wild, but they had no time to stop and little inclination, given their pursuer.

He had come out of nowhere, again and again, striking fast and hard and refusing to die despite their best efforts. The worst of it, to Mervin's thinking, was that they still had no idea who he was. He was a blank, a wild card dealt into the game by an unknown player. That lack of identification made him all the more terrifying to Mervin. Who was he? Why had he chosen to interfere?

There were possibilities, of course—suppositions, backed up by the smallest shreds of evidence. The man had military-issue hardware, but his uniform bore no identifying markers. The accent was American, but again, that was no guarantee of anything. Mervin himself was American, working for a German-based organization.

Was he working for a rival organization? The Society of Thylea had many enemies—their activities had brought annoyance to a variety of criminal operations, and there were, of course, the requisite rival occult groups....

Mervin contemplated the world of shadows and fog of which he had long been a part. Secret societies had always been the province of the wealthy and bored, and that had not changed. The Society of Thylea was made up of rich old men, as were the upper echelons of their rival organizations. Race, gender and age were variable factors, but wealth and boredom were always present. Stupidity, as well—money might be the grease for global gears, but it was not power in and of itself. Neither was a cobbled-together ideology, no matter how attractive to the mentally deficient.

But money could buy men. It had bought Mervin, and perhaps it had bought the man who seemed determined to kill them. Was that it, then—money, rather than nationalism or patriotism? Was that the lever?

"Stop mumbling so loud," Kraft murmured. Mervin glared at him. They were both squatting behind a jagged outcropping close to the river. The stone seemed to radiate cold and Mervin's thin frame was racked with shivers. Behind them, the others were spread out, their camouflage gear helping them to blend in with their surroundings. They had pulled the rafts ashore not far downriver and covered them with camouflage netting. It had been their intent to make camp. Instead, they were crouching in hiding.

While planning the operation, Mervin had made a thorough analysis of various points along the Noatak River, and had chosen several adequate campsites, should such be required. With the attack, and Kraft's idiotic offer of a raft, they'd been forced to bypass the sites chosen by Mervin, sacrificing the plan in favor of speed. Now they were low on fuel and supplies, and the place they had chosen to put ashore was seemingly already occupied.

"Who are they?" Mervin asked, reaching for the binoculars that Kraft was peering through. Kraft swatted his groping hand and said, "Campers, by the look of them."

"What are they doing?"

"Offhand, I'd say they're camping, Mervin. That's what campers do."

"There shouldn't be any campers out here," Mervin snapped, hunkering down behind the outcropping. He fumbled for a cigarette and Kraft clamped a hand over his.

"Maybe not, yet there they are, nonetheless, between us and our objective. We must adapt and persevere as our ancestors did in the time of upheaval, when their empire crumbled and they were forced to share their world with beasts." Kraft took his eyes away from the binoculars and looked at him. "Adapt, Mervin."

Mervin jerked his hand away. He stuffed one of his remaining cigarettes in his mouth and grunted. "Boyd's dead," he said.

"Yes. Otherwise, he would have joined us by now." Kraft sniffed. "I could have told you that little scheme wasn't going to work. Perhaps if I had been the one to stay behind, but Boyd was obviously no match for our pursuer."

"You could have mentioned that," Mervin snapped.

"I assumed you would reach that conclusion yourself," Kraft said mildly. His tone grew hard as he added, "I also assumed that once we were in the field you would not countermand my orders. Now we are down a man we could ill afford to lose because you disregarded my command."

Mervin met his cold gaze truculently. "We have enough."

"Barely, and we haven't even reached HYPER-BOREA yet." Kraft sighed. "And we left most of the supplies back at our last camp." He smiled crookedly. "Our uninvited guest really did a number on us."

Mervin lit his cigarette. "They have food."

Kraft looked at him. The simple statement of fact had a sinister undercurrent.

"You said we were running low on supplies. They have supplies. Ergo, we take theirs." Mervin blinked and then it was his turn to smile. "Even better, we take them."

"Hostages," Kraft said and his disgust was evident.

"We have taken hostages before, when it suited our purposes. They are necessary. They will give us an advantage. Take them," he said.

Kraft stared at him. Mervin blinked slowly, owlishly. "Take them," he said again. "As you pointed out, we are running low on warm bodies. There are some bodies over there. Take them in the name of Thylea."

For a moment, Mervin thought the other man might refuse. But pragmatism, as ever, prevailed. Kraft slunk back toward the others. Mervin watched him go and sucked speculatively on his cigarette. Kraft was becoming hard to live with. Something was affecting his good sense. Mervin wondered if he would have to dispatch the big man sooner than anticipated.

A moment later he discarded the thought. He had no friends here, save Kraft. Too, their opponent remained at large, hunting them. He was a devil, a fury, hounding them for their crimes. No, killing Kraft now would only put him at a disadvantage.

Kraft and the others crept past him like sinister shadows, moving with a speed and stealth that unnerved Mervin. His hand found his pistol, and then his cigarettes. He wondered if the hikers would have any. He hoped so. This endeavor had been stressful, and he was running low. At the rate things were going, he'd be getting the cravings before they got back to civilization.

An automatic rifle snarled and someone screamed. Mervin huddled against the rock, glaring at the river over the cherry-red tip of his cigarette. He hated the river. He was cold and wet all the time. But it had to be this way. Whoever had designed the installation had done a good job. It was unlikely to be discovered by accident and would be hard to locate even for dedicated searchers. Back when the base had been occupied, the surrounding area had been wilderness. There had likely been roving patrols sweeping the river and the nearby trails for intruders. Now there were just hikers.

Mervin smiled as he heard Kraft shout. He poked his head up over the edge of the rock and saw that they had the camp well in hand. Kraft could be quite efficient when he put his mind to it. Mervin stood and strolled into the camp, hands in the pockets of his coat. "How many?" he asked.

"Four of them," Kraft said. He gestured at the three men and one woman who now sat huddled about their breakfast fire, faces tense and wary. One of them, a young black man, had a darkening bruise on his face—a preemptive warning. Mervin glanced from the young man to Kraft, who shrugged. "He resisted."

"I have no doubt," Mervin said. He looked at the others—there were five of them, besides him and Kraft. Heinrich, Adams, Picher, Goetz and Burke; Adams was English, Burke and Picher were American and Heinrich and Goetz were German. A multinational assortment of murderers, Mervin thought, and bent down to scoop a strip of bacon out of a pan. He held his cigarette as he chewed methodically. "They are really campers, then?"

"I have no doubt," Kraft said, throwing his earlier words at him.

"Good. I will explain the situation to them." Mervin sank to his haunches and looked at their captives, his mind processing facts—three white, one black; three men and one woman; mid-twenties to early thirties. Their gear was new and high-end. Young professionals on a retreat, he surmised. Pleased with himself, he puffed on his cigarette and said, "Gentlemen and lady, you will have noticed the men with guns. They will kill you if you attempt to run. They will kill you if you attempt to resist. If I tell them to, they will kill you. Draw your own conclusions as to the limits of your freedom. You are prisoners of the Society of Thylea, and as such you may take heart that your captivity will be short and painless." He stepped closer and sniffed. "One of you smokes. You will give me your cigarettes."

The woman cleared her throat nervously. "I—I

don't have any. I'm trying to—to quit. All I have is the patch."

Before anyone could react, Mervin grabbed her by the hair and dragged her away from the others. Holding her by her scalp, he snarled, "You are lying. I can smell the tar on you. Give them to me, or I will hurt you."

"Leave her alone," the black man growled, making to rise to his feet. Kraft struck him quickly and forcefully, chopping him expertly on the back of the neck. The young man flopped down with a groan. The other two, who had been in the midst of rising, as well, froze.

"They will kill you if you attempt to resist," Mervin reiterated. He looked back at the woman and tightened his grip. "Cigarettes—where."

"Mervin, let her go," Kraft said.

"Give them to me." Mervin shook her hard enough to cause her jaws to click. She flung out a hand, indicating one of the tents, tears streaming down her features.

"I was just—I couldn't—I didn't…" she wailed. Mervin slapped her and let her fall.

"Shut up," he said. His voice was once more a calm monotone. Addicts were all the same, regardless of the addiction. He went to the tent, ransacked it and found a pack of filtered cigarettes. Pinching the filter off one, he shoved it into his mouth and lit it. Kraft was waiting for him as he stepped out.

"Are you finished?" the big man asked.

"For now," Mervin said.

"Was this because you actually had a plan, or because you needed your nicotine fix?" Kraft demanded. Mervin stared at him for a moment.

"I always have a plan, Kraft," he said. "You would do well to remember that."

18

Bolan balanced the laminated map on his knees as the motorized raft trundled along the river. The Noatak wasn't as wild as some rivers Bolan had traversed, but it wasn't exactly a Sunday afternoon leisure trip. He estimated that Kraft and the others were only a few hours ahead. The Society of Thylea soldiers had left behind most of their supplies, which meant they were having to stop sooner and waste time locating food. Bolan had found the remains of an improvised fish snare and several trench fires when he and Blackjack had made camp. Thanks to their quarry's supplies, Bolan and Blackjack had all the food they needed.

Mervin's two rafts were also weighed down with at least seven men, explosives and other equipment. Blackjack was no lightweight, but she was nowhere near as heavy as a fully armed terrorist. Bolan had been pushing the motorized raft as hard as he dared to make the most of their advantage.

Another day, maybe two, Bolan thought, tracing a line on the map with one finger. Longer, possibly, if the coordinates Ackroyd and Ferguson had provided were off somehow. He still wasn't certain how to eliminate the threat HYPERBOREA posed, after

Kraft and the others were dealt with. Explosives would be the most efficient means, but that'd run the risk of releasing the very thing he wanted to bury forever.

He looked up. Blackjack crouched at the front of the raft. She had been casting a look back at him the entire time he'd been getting his bearings. By the fourth such glance, Bolan started to get annoyed. "What?" he asked.

"Why'd he leave the raft?" she said, frowning. "Why not disable it?"

For a moment Bolan didn't reply. In truth, he'd been wondering the same thing himself for the past two days. The trip had been made mostly in silence; Blackjack had spoken little since killing Bolan's attacker. She didn't seem unduly bothered by it, but it was hard to tell. This was the first time she'd outright asked him anything since that night.

"He wants to fight me," he said.

"So he's suicidal?"

The Executioner smiled slightly. "I've met men like him before. They need challenge the way you and I need air. They pit themselves against dangerous opponents and relish the pain that follows." He scratched his chin. "A nastier sort of adrenaline junkie, I guess you could call them."

"I flew one of them 'man versus wild' types out here one time," she said, not looking at him. "He wanted to be dropped off in nothing but some clothes he'd hand-made with a stone knife and an ax. He paid me good money, too." She met his amused gaze and smirked. "His wife paid me to go find him when he didn't turn up where he was supposed to."

"Did you?"

"More or less," she said. Her smirk faded. "He near about froze to death."

Bolan looked at her. "He must have been thankful."

"Not so you'd notice," she said, turning away.

"Thank you, by the way," Bolan said.

"For what?"

"Saving me," he said. "I didn't say it properly before."

She shrugged. "You'd have handled it, I expect."

"Possibly, but you showed up at the right time. So… thank you."

"First time I ever killed a man," she said, so softly he almost didn't hear it. Bolan carefully folded his map and stuck it back into a pocket.

"The first time is always the hardest," he said.

"You've done it plenty, I expect." Water splashed up over the side of the raft, slopping between them. Bolan blinked spray out of his eyes and nodded tersely.

"I've done it when I had to."

"You keep track?"

Bolan hesitated. "No," he said, after a moment.

She grunted. "That many, then?"

Bolan fell silent. She wasn't far off. In his War Everlasting, he'd killed more men than he liked to consider. "I've never killed a man who didn't deserve it," he said finally.

"And these guys—they deserve it?"

"Oh, yeah," Bolan said.

"Good." She shook herself and smiled grimly. "I didn't feel guilty, you know. But I was wondering whether I should've."

"Ms. Blackjack—Ida—the day you need to worry is the day you stop wondering," Bolan said. He looked up at the sky. It was getting dark. "We'll find a place to make camp and settle down for the night."

Blackjack leaned forward. "That's— Hey! Looks like somebody is in trouble!" She glanced back at him. "There's a guy out there, hip-deep in the river, trying to flag us down. Looks like he needs help," she said.

"Maybe, maybe not," Bolan said. He cursed. His instincts were screaming "trap," but whether it was or not, it was a delay. Nonetheless, if someone was in trouble, Bolan couldn't turn a blind eye. "Get back here and take the raft in. They haven't seen me yet." He unholstered his Desert Eagle and pressed it into her hand. "Just in case," he said.

"What are you going to do?"

"I'm going to make sure everything is on the up and up. Take the raft in and see what he wants from us, but if anything funny happens, try not to get shot."

"You got a comforting way with words, Cooper."

"So I've been told." Bolan slipped into the river. Holding tight to the side of the raft, he allowed it to pull him along for a bit before letting go and submerging himself. The water was cold, but Bolan was used to it. Carefully and quickly, he made his way to the rocky shore. As Blackjack took the raft toward the distant figure, he slithered out of the water and into the brush. Scanning his surroundings briefly, Bolan moved into the trees. He could smell a campfire and cooking beans. He moved closer to the camp. There were two tents and a fire crackling merrily. Three people sat around the fire, their body language and faces betraying a bone-deep fear.

Quietly, he began to circle the camp. Some instinct caused him to freeze in midcreep and he hunched low against the ground, peering intently at a lump of brush. The Executioner's eyes narrowed as he saw the briefest flash of movement. An improvised ghillie suit; Bolan was almost impressed. He faded back into the scrub as noiselessly as a cat.

The raft's motor had cut off, and he heard the sound of voices—Blackjack's and someone else's. Would they have left just one—no. Bolan willed himself to absolute stillness as he spotted the second man, moving between the tents. His rifle was slung, and he had a pistol in his hands. He stepped out with his weapon raised as Blackjack was led into the camp. "Freeze, bitch," he snarled. He froze for a moment, as he realized that Bolan was nowhere to be seen. "Where is he?"

"Where's who?" Blackjack said. She raised her hands. "You wouldn't happen to have the keys to my plane, would you?"

"Shut up!" the gunman snapped. "Where is he? Where's the bastard at?"

"Only bastard I see is the one in front of me," Blackjack said. The gunman reached her in one quick stride and struck her in the belly. She folded over and sank to her knees. Bolan tensed, but he couldn't move until he knew for certain there were only two of them. Hold on, Ida, he thought. He flexed his fingers. The one in front of him hadn't moved. They were smart enough for that, at least.

"Where is he?" the gunman snarled, grabbing a handful of her hair. The man who'd led her into camp—a young black man—started forward, but backed off as the gunman waved his weapon at him. "Get over there with the others, now!"

The one in the ghillie suit shifted slightly, tracking the young man as he sat down. There were a fair few black eyes and bruises spread among the group; the campers, whoever they were, weren't helping by choice.

Blackjack wheezed and began to climb to her feet. As she came up, her hand moved behind her back, beneath her coat, and reappeared with Bolan's Desert Eagle. The gunman cursed and stepped back in surprise, his own weapon coming up. Both pistols went off at once. Blackjack went over backward and Bolan's heart sank. He'd waited too long. He lunged at the camouflaged killer, and landed square on his back. Bolan's knees dug into the man's spine and his hands snaked around his head. The man bucked and began to struggle, clawing at Bolan's hands.

Bolan gave a rapid jerk and the man's neck snapped. Their struggles had alerted the other gunman, however, and he scrambled toward the fire, his pistol growling out several shots at the scrub where Bolan was. Or rather, where Bolan had been, for the Executioner was already on his feet, the dead man's AR-15 in his hands. He sprang from the brush and hit the ground, shoulder first, rolling to his feet even as his weapon lit up the gloom, spitting death.

The gunman gave a cry but didn't stop. He crashed through the campfire and into the campers, who tried to get out of the way. One of them wasn't quick enough and the young man yelped as the wounded killer slid behind him, laced an arm around his neck and pressed his pistol to the side of his head. "Stop, stop or I kill him!" the killer howled.

"No," Bolan said. He pivoted, firing at the campfire. Hot embers and ash sprayed up, catching both men. The camper yelped and twisted, as did his captor. They swayed apart, just for an instant. Bolan took the shot. He fired once, and the gunman fell back, face a red ruin. Bolan waited, counting to ten. When no other enemies presented themselves, he went to check on Blackjack.

He crouched beside her and reached for her wrist. Her eyes popped open and the Desert Eagle swung up. Bolan twisted aside and caught her wrist, shoving the pistol away from his face. "Whoa!"

She coughed and he helped her sit up. "Are you hit?" he asked, not quite able to believe his eyes. She shook her head and tugged at a hole in her thick coat.

"Didn't even come close," she wheezed.

"You have a funny definition of close," he said, helping her to her feet. He turned to look at the campers. One of the young men was hugging the woman. The other two were looking at him as if afraid they had traded one set of captors for another. "Folks, I'm with the Justice Department," Bolan said. "You're safe now."

He questioned them quickly. They knew nothing, beyond that a group of men had surprised them earlier in the day, taken them hostage and forced them to act as bait for him and Blackjack. Bolan knew that it had been nothing more than a delaying tactic. It was a stall, meant to slow him down. And it had. Kraft and the others were likely already at HYPERBOREA. He hefted the AR-15 and checked the magazine then he looked at the group of frightened people. "Do any of you have a phone?"

One of the men nodded. "We brought it for emergencies."

"I'd say this qualifies. I'm going to give you a number. I want you to call it as soon as I'm gone, and tell the person who answers that Striker is making his play. They'll ask for your coordinates, and I want you to give them as clearly as you can. Then sit tight and wait." He looked at Blackjack and added, "That goes for you, too."

"What? But—" she began. He took the Desert Eagle from her and checked the magazine before holstering it. He went to the body of the first man he'd killed and snagged an extra magazine for the AR-15.

"But nothing," Bolan said. He tossed her the rifle and the magazine and picked up the rifle the gunman had dropped in his rush toward the hostages. "You're staying here. That close call was your last."

"And what about you?" Blackjack demanded.

"I'm taking the raft." Bolan met her angry gaze and said, "You've gone above and beyond, Ida. But from here on out, I've got to go it alone."

19

"Hurry up and get the rafts tied off!" Kraft bellowed, shouting to be heard over the crash of water spilling across the rocks. Kraft looked over at Mervin, who stared at the slithering waterfall with wide eyes. "What is it?"

"The government made this reservoir," Mervin said absently. HYPERBOREA was a great skeleton of a place, all red-tinted metal painted in weatherproof paint. It was situated just so in the side of a crag that curved upward from the river like a sharp fang of rock. The waterfall ensured that it was partially hidden by a curtain of water, which pounded down from somewhere above and smashed into the deep waters of the small lake that spread out around the research base.

"Like a moat, yes, so you said. They had to displace the water to get back into the cave systems," Kraft said, passing up a satchel to one of his men who climbed a rusty ladder. The ladder rose from the dark water and up into the web of struts and girders that acted as the structural support for the bulk of the facility. Above the ladder was a wide gantry that led to a heavy bulkhead which was, if Mervin was to be believed, the entrance to HYPERBOREA.

"That's not supposed to be there," Mervin said hesitantly, gesturing at the waterfall. Kraft looked at it more closely. The upper reaches of the crag had that peculiar look some rocks got, like a loaf of bread that had too much baking soda added to the mix. The rocks had been forced aside by several decades of water pressure, and the whole crag had a loose look that Kraft instinctively didn't like.

"Well, it's here, and there's nothing we can do about it," he said.

Mervin shoved a cigarette into his mouth and looked at him. "Can't you feel it? This whole place is unstable. It's coming apart."

"As long as it holds together while we get what we came for, I don't particularly care," Kraft said, passing up another satchel. The ladder whined as his men climbed up and down. A loud groan of straining metal drifted down from above, and everyone froze in place. Kraft expelled a breath and said, "Hop to it, gentlemen. We're on a clock."

"I knew the structure would likely be unsound, but I never expected…" Mervin's face was white and his expression was strained. He shook his head, scattering ash from his cigarette. "There's no guarantee that the quarantine is even still functional."

"If not, wouldn't we already be sick? We've been heading upriver. If there was contamination, we would have already begun vomiting out our intestines, no?" Kraft said, clapping Mervin on the shoulder. Mervin twitched away.

"It's not safe," he said. "If we use the explosives, this whole structure could collapse!"

"It's your plan, Mervin."

"I know! But there are variables I was not aware of!"

"Yes, that is becoming a habit with you, eh?" Kraft said harshly.

Mervin whipped around to glare at him. "What?"

"You heard me," Kraft said. "This whole affair has been riddled with problems. You seem to have taken little of your usual care in crafting your schemes this time. Usually you are so precise…but this time, your mistakes may cost us everything."

Mervin's cigarette drooped. Kraft snatched it and flung it aside. "You and your damn cigarettes and your petty, precise little plans," he said. He could feel the others watching but for once he didn't care. Mervin had pushed him too far. He was tired of the little man's weaknesses and his constant whining and complaining. "Why did you come, Mervin? This would have been easier without you."

"You needed me," Mervin snapped.

"Did we? Or did you simply want to think we did? Did you see your use coming to an end, Mervin? The ascension of Thylea looms, and the Tick-Tock Man is frightened because he is suddenly no longer necessary. It will be a new world, born from the ashes of the old. A world where only the strongest can survive, where a man's blood and the power in it are all the advantage he will need. That frightens you, doesn't it, Mervin? Or maybe you felt the need to prove yourself, eh?" Kraft eyed him. "That's why I agreed to let you come, after all."

Mervin stared at him, and for the first time, Kraft had no problem telling what the little man was thinking. He smiled. "Hate makes us strong. Now get up the ladder."

Mervin did as he was told, and without complaint, which was suspicious. When Kraft reached the gantry, he grabbed Picher by the shoulder and handed the man his remaining magazines of ammunition. "Here, take these. I want you in among those struts. Our nameless friend will be along shortly. See that he has some difficulty, eh?"

"You think he'll get past the others?" Picher asked, doubtfully.

Kraft shrugged and looked out at the river. "I think we can't rely on things working according to plan. Do what you can. Don't get cocky." He clapped Picher on the shoulder and turned to see Mervin glaring at him. He had heard the exchange. Kraft didn't particularly care. "Heinrich, Adams, get the explosives out. We've wasted too much time as it is—"

The structure shuddered. Kraft staggered but immediately righted himself. Metal groaned and from somewhere within the nest of struts, he heard rivets pop and rattle. Mervin's glare vanished as panic replaced anger. "We have to get out of here!" he shouted, stumbling in Kraft's direction. "I won't die here! It's not worth it!"

Kraft caught him easily by the throat and propelled him backward, toward the bulkhead. "Not worth it? Those are not the words of a hero, Mervin. Those are not the words of a man whose companions have perished on a mighty quest." He slammed the smaller man against the bulkhead and tapped the keypad set into the frame. Inside the bulkhead was a thick hatch, resembling a submarine portal. "I assume the correct code would unlock the hatch, yes? Too bad we failed to get Ackroyd." He leaned close to Mervin. "Best laid plans, eh?" He released the little man and turned to the others. "Explosives—now."

"Wait, we should think about this—consider the variables," Mervin began. Kraft held a finger to his lips, silencing him.

"He who dares, wins."

They had salvaged most, though not all, of their explosives. As his men set them up, Kraft went through the other satchels. They had the biohazard suits as well as the containment units. As far as tools went, those were the most important.

It took Heinrich and Adams only a few minutes to set the explosives, which consisted of C-4 in shaped charges. The explosion was to be contained as much as possible. Mervin had foreseen that the structure would be too dilapidated to withstand a major explosion, even if he hadn't correctly gauged the extent of said decay.

Kraft clasped his hands behind his back and nodded as Adams looked at him. "Blow it," he said.

The explosion, when it came, wasn't loud. The hatch was blown off its hinges and fell with a thunderous crash, shaking the gantry. An echoing moan emanated from the surrounding structure, and rocks fell from above, splashing down perilously close to their rafts.

Above, a strut gave way and fell, brushing hard against the gantry and nearly tossing Kraft from his feet. He maintained his balance and waved smoke and dust out of his face. Behind the blasted hatch, a corridor bathed in dim emergency lighting was revealed. The sterile, slightly damp stink of quarantine greeted his nostrils and he gagged. Mervin, wide-eyed, was looking around like a mouse watching for eagles.

Kraft grabbed him. "Let's go."

"The bags," Mervin said hollowly.

"What?" Kraft turned and cursed. The satchels containing the hazard suits were gone, knocked from the gantry by the falling strut. Kraft closed his eyes and rubbed his chin. "It doesn't matter," he said. "There will be containers within."

"And if not?" Mervin asked, glaring at him. "What then, huh? What do we do then, Kraft? Since my plans are so faulty, where is yours, eh? Where is your stratagem for this?"

"We adapt, Mervin. We persevere." Kraft matched the other man's glare with one of his own and said, "Even if that means I must carry that damned disease back to civilization myself, even if I must be the tip of the spear, to plunge death into the heart of the world, I will do so."

Mervin jerked back as if stung. The others nodded in agreement as the gantry trembled beneath their feet. The weight of destiny pressed hard upon the facility. It pressed hard upon them, as well. He looked at Picher. "You know what to do?"

The man nodded. *"Vril-YA,"* he said loudly.

"Vril-YA," Kraft replied, and the others said it with him, even Mervin.

He was so close he could taste it. Kraft could feel the brittle scrape of the wolf-wind on his soul. Everything he was, everything he had done, had led to this moment, this stretch of tainted metal and the dark sickness nestled within. "Come, my friends," he said. "We can't keep the end of the world waiting."

20

As he stared up at HYPERBOREA, Bolan had to admit that Ackroyd's description hadn't been far off. The base had obviously been constructed around the skeleton of an oil rig, likely airlifted from the Arctic Ocean. He spotted the rafts easily. They'd been tied up at the bottom of the structure amongst the lattice-work of support struts, beneath a rust-riddled ladder.

Bolan guided his raft toward the others, his every muscle tense with anticipation. The pounding of the waterfall was loud, echoing around him and filling the air with spray. As he slid into the nest of struts, he caught the clang of metal on metal. An assault rifle roared a moment later, but Bolan was already diving over the side into the icy water. He had expected an ambush, and his enemies had not disappointed him.

He dove deep, his lungs burning. The water was cold and it cut through him like a knife. It was hard to see because the water was filthy with rust and oil and other less identifiable things. Nonetheless, he swam for the ladder, which extended well below the water-line. He grabbed the closest rung and began to climb. Bolan raised his head above the water and scanned his surroundings. The raft he'd just abandoned was sinking, perforated by the ambush.

Swiftly, he pulled himself out of the water and began to climb. The ladder rattled and shuddered beneath his weight. Speed was his only ally until he reached the walkways above. The unseen AR-15 opened up again, growling out a deadly song. Bullets struck the ladder and struts around Bolan, causing him to jerk and twist in an attempt to avoid being struck. Bolan cursed as he heard the pop of age and environment-weakened bolts from somewhere above him. The ladder began to bend and sway as he continued to climb.

Bolan knew in an instant that he wasn't going to make it. Metal squealed and screeched and popped with gunshot rhythm and then he was falling backward, still holding tight to the ladder. His gut lurched and the world spun about him as he was forced back and down. The ruptured end of the ladder struck a strut and became lodged in place and Bolan found himself dangling above the water. His shoulders blazed with pain from the force of the sudden stop, but he held grimly to the rust-weakened rungs.

Boots clanged on metal. The Executioner craned his neck and looked up. His assailant approached carefully, climbing across the top of the collapsed ladder. "Lucky, lucky man," he grunted. "You did for the others, but it looks like your luck has run out."

Bolan twisted in place. Pain ran the length of his arm as he lost his grip on one of the rungs and was forced to dangle one-handed. He glared up at the gunman as the man inched closer and took aim with his weapon. "They'll reward me for this," he said.

"Don't count on it yet," Bolan snarled. Before his enemy could react, Bolan's hand flashed down and he snatched his KA-BAR combat knife from its sheath and stabbed it through the man's boot and the ankle beneath. The gunman screamed as Bolan jerked the blade free and he fell heavily onto the ladder, losing his weapon to the waters below. Bolan grabbed one of his thrashing arms and yanked on it, hard, hearing the distinct "pop" of the man's arm dislocating. The ladder whined as it began to come loose from its temporary mooring. Bolan hauled himself up and onto the shaking ladder. He had to move quickly. Ignoring the agonized thrashing of his would-be assassin, Bolan clambered over him, knife in hand. He had just managed to reach the closest strut as a flailing hand fastened onto his foot. Bolan turned and drove his other foot into the man's face. Bone crunched. The force of the blow shook the ladder loose and it tumbled down, taking its wounded burden with it. The man's scream spiraled up as he hit the water and then ceased abruptly.

Breathing heavily, Bolan pushed himself to his feet. He waited a moment to see if the man would surface. When he didn't, Bolan moved around the gantry toward the entrance to the facility. It was wide open, and he could see the black marks of a small explosion.

"Plan B," he said. Carefully, Bolan ducked through the open hatch and stepped into HYPERBOREA. The first thing he noticed was the smell. It stank of damp and rust, and the air had a greasy solidity to it. He moved through the dimly lit corridor. Emergency lighting had come on the minute the door was opened, and it flickered and pulsed weakly. That the system was still functioning despite decades of neglect was impressive. They had built things to last back then. I wonder for how much longer, though, Bolan thought. He drew the Desert Eagle and checked it carefully. The holster was waterproof, and it hadn't been submerged for long, but there was no telling whether or not he could rely on it. Holding it close, he continued on, alert for any indication of another ambush—he knew that besides Kraft and Mervin, there were only two men left, which still put the odds at 4-1. Better than 5-1, he thought.

Bolan had no trouble traversing the maze of corridors, having memorized the blueprints for the base on the flight out from Seattle. HYPERBOREA was a compact labyrinth, with the outer corridors leading to the galley and the sleeping quarters and the inner area housing workstations. The central rig area, where a pipeline would have been before the base was repurposed, was now a shaft shot directly into the guts of the mountain. That was where they'd found it, Ackroyd had said.

As he traversed the base, Bolan wondered how they'd come across Ymir in the first place. Had some adventurous outdoorsman stumbled across a sign of what would become an archaeological site and made a report? And why had the Feds become involved in the first place? No answers had been forthcoming in the files he'd been given. He suspected that Ackroyd himself hadn't really known.

At any rate, it didn't matter now. It existed, and it was a problem the Executioner would have to solve. The sound of voices came to him, and he froze.

"Get it open, Mervin. Thylea calls to us," Kraft said.

"It will take a few minutes to break the code," Mervin replied. "We can't risk blowing it open. Patience is a virtue, as you have said to me many times."

Kraft grunted. "Go check on Picher. See what those gunshots were about."

Bolan pressed himself flat against the wall as footsteps sounded farther up the corridor. He looked at the heavy pipes that lined the ceiling. The corridor wasn't very wide and, reaching up, he planted a palm on one wall and then did the same against the other. His feet went next as he wedged himself upward in among the pipes. It was an uncomfortable fit, but he was only planning to hold it for a few moments. He couldn't allow them to get into that lab.

The footsteps got louder. Two men rounded the corner, weapons held loosely. One, who was more alert than the other, happened to glance up at the last moment. His mouth opened even as Bolan dropped onto them. The Executioner landed between them with a clang and his leg snapped out in a side kick, catching the inobservant one in the back of the knees and sending him sprawling. Bolan's fist struck the other in the groin, bending him double with a shrill wheeze.

In the tight confines of the corridor, Bolan twisted, reaching up to grab the bending gunman by his scalp and jaw as he hooked the throat of the other with his ankles. His shoulders tensed and heaved and the first man's neck bone gave a sharp snap as it split in two. Bolan used his legs to haul the second man, who was thrashing desperately, back within reach. Then, with a ruthless efficiency, he repeated the maneuver and snapped the man's neck with a single, powerful twist.

"Oh, bravo, my friend," Kraft said, clapping.

"Bravo, indeed. But I am certain you do not need me to tell you how impressive you are."

Bolan rose slowly to his feet. He flexed his hands as he eyed Kraft, considering. Kraft smiled, as if he could guess what the Executioner was thinking. "I knew you were out here, somewhere. It was the only reason Picher would have fired." He looked past Bolan at the dead men. His smile slipped slightly. "It will be a bitter victory, I think. You have delayed the inevitable and cost us many heroes, my unknown friend. Tell me your name so that I might know who I send to dine with the gods of the Aryan peoples...."

"In the past I was called the Executioner," Bolan said.

Kraft laughed in obvious delight. "Oh, how wonderful," he said. "Do you hear, Mervin?" He hesitated. "Mervin?" he said again. There was no answer. Kraft glanced back. Bolan slid forward like a striking snake, the Desert Eagle springing into his hand. Kraft spun around, and his forearm crashed against the barrel even as it fired. The roar of the pistol was loud in the confined space. Kraft's palm struck Bolan's wrist and the pistol was sent clattering away. The big man's other fist snapped out and his knuckles slammed up against the bottom of Bolan's chin, nearly taking his feet out from under him. Bolan stepped back and rubbed his aching jaw as Kraft glided after him.

"Do you know what they called me, back in the service? *Sturmvogel*—'the Storm Eagle.' A very colorful name, and one I wore with pride. I was a great soldier, but now I serve a higher power. Who do you serve, Executioner?" Kraft said. His trench knife seemed to appear in his hand as if by magic and the blade hissed as it cut the air. Bolan backed away and drew his own knife.

"I fight for justice," he said.

Kraft snickered. "What a coincidence—so do I!"

They crept toward one another, blades bared, arms raised in mirrored stances. "The justice of a better world," Kraft went on. "The justice of a fairer time, when strength and blood meant more—"

"Shut up," Bolan said. They clashed in a lightning-snap of blades and muscle, knife edges scraping against one another. Bolan bent to the side and his foot shot out, catching Kraft in the hip. Kraft's hand slammed down and his fingers dug into Bolan's calf painfully. They went over in a tangle of knees and elbows. Bolan felt his lip burst, and his vision sparked as a fist graced his temple. His forearm caught Kraft in the throat. The big man shot backward, gagging, and Bolan hit him with a shoulder in the belly. They crashed against the wall and Kraft caught him by the sides and bodily flung him away. Breathing heavily, they eyed one another.

Bolan raised his blade. A thin line of Kraft's blood crawled across the knife. Kraft touched his side and grimaced. "I knew you were good," he wheezed. He showed his own blade. It was smeared with red. "But then, so am I."

The Executioner winced. He touched his side and his fingertips came away wet. It hurt when he breathed. His fingers curled into a fist and he moved forward. His blow hissed over Kraft's shoulder, and his knife sliced up, cutting through coat and flesh. Kraft grunted and snapped his head forward. Bolan saw stars and staggered back. Kraft *was* good.

Kraft came in at a charge, his heavy tread echoing in the corridor. A moment before he reached Bolan, the latter realized the noise he'd heard wasn't an echo. The corridor seemed to bulge and shimmy and both men nearly lost their balance. Kraft braced himself against the wall and looked around, eyes narrowed. "Shit," he said.

Bolan found his feet and lunged, throwing himself into the other man shoulder first even as HYPERBOREA gave another, louder groan. They hit the floor as the sound of tearing metal filled the air. Bolan had to get past him. There was no telling where Mervin was. He could have already gotten to Ymir while Bolan had been busy with Kraft. Bolan grabbed Kraft's head and bounced it off the floor. Kraft twitched and went limp. The Executioner scooped up his pistol and hurried down the corridor, wasting no more time on the big man.

The base was beginning to shift around him. Pipes rattled and several burst, hosing the corridor with rusty, ice-cold water. Bolan pressed on, one arm held up to shield his face. The persistent whine of an alarm gave a strangled squawk and went silent. The floor trembled beneath his feet, as if the base were coming apart at the seams. The explosion they'd used to breach the base had obviously set off a long-delayed structural collapse. That meant Bolan no longer had to figure out how to destroy the base, but he still had to make sure the base's secrets died with it.

He rounded a corner and saw the markings that indicated the research laboratory. The hatch was open, and Bolan's heart went cold. He moved closer, Desert Eagle held low.

Bolan paused in front of the open hatch. He smelled cigarette smoke. A moment later the Executioner heard the click of a pistol being cocked.

21

"Don't move! I will kill you if you move," Mervin said. "Hand me your weapon slowly, if you please."

He took the Desert Eagle from Bolan's hand and stuffed it into his coat. The little man gestured. "Inside, please," he said. Bolan hesitated. "It's quite safe, I assure you. By my calculations, this contagion requires constant fuel to propagate itself. That's why it kills so quickly. It was easy enough to extrapolate its limitations from what little information I was able to find. It took eight days from the point of discovery for the first case of infection to occur, and then, only after the *corpus* was autopsied. Ackroyd himself is likely not sure, after all this time, how it happened. I theorize that the initial infection required contamination—a bit like a vampire reinvigorated by a taste of warm, fresh blood. But when the blood ran out, well, Ymir went back to sleep. And it will sleep still, until I choose to awaken it. Inside, please."

"And then what?" Bolan said, stepping through the hatch. "You'll kill a couple million innocent people?"

Mervin laughed. "Hardly. Let Thylea stay in the mythic past where it belongs. I have better plans." He smiled. "I knew you'd beat Kraft. I knew you'd come after me. I knew the open hatch would hold your attention for the 6.7 seconds I needed to get a gun to your head." He jerked his chin. "Look at it."

The body lay on an examination table, curled into a ball within its plastic shroud. He could just make out the brown, withered shape of its form. It really was a mummy. "The mummy's curse," Mervin said, and giggled. The chill in Bolan's chest grew, and his skin prickled.

He looked at Mervin and the little man's chuckle died in his throat. "No," Mervin said, as if Bolan had spoken, "No, it's not funny, is it? It's quite frightening, when considered from an emotional standpoint. But I'm not emotional. I'm a rational man, logical, and this is a treasure trove. Move back. Move back, please." Mervin gesticulated with the pistol. Bolan, hands spread, did as the little man indicated. Even as he did so, his mind was awash with calculations of his own—Mervin was keeping himself well out of reach, but not so far away as to give Bolan enough distance to avoid a shot. "I don't know who you are or why you've seen fit to interfere, but it's done. You are done."

"They know who you are, Mervin," Bolan said. The base shuddered again, and the emergency lighting flickered. Mervin looked around nervously. "There are Federal agents already moving into position. There's no way you're making it off this river, let alone Alaska. If you surrender now—"

"I'll go into a dark hole and disappear," Mervin said. He smiled. "I've worked with conspiracy nuts long enough to know there is a grain of truth to it all.

Governments make people disappear all the time. Especially when they know things they shouldn't."

Bolan said nothing. Truthfully, he couldn't say what would happen to Mervin if he surrendered. More than likely, he'd be pumped for information about the Society of Thylea, dumped into a hole somewhere and kept without trial. He was a terrorist, and he'd be treated as such.

"I do intend to disappear—never fear," Mervin said. Bolan recognized the signs of a man talking just to hear himself. He looked at the thing on the table. It was small to be so dangerous. "Once I get what I came for."

Need to keep him talking, Bolan thought. The longer Mervin talked, the better the chance Bolan could take him down. "And what's that? It's not like you can risk walking out of here with its skull tucked under your arm. And it doesn't look like you brought any containment equipment."

Mervin's face twisted into a grimace. "No matter," he said. "I can improvise something." He looked at the counters that lined the walls, as if searching for something to hold his prize. Just then, the base shook again and Bolan seized his moment. He slapped the barrel of the .22 aside, even as Mervin convulsively pulled the trigger. Bolan's palm caught Mervin in the throat and he staggered back, gagging. He retained hold of his weapon and flailed about, pulling the trigger again. Bolan ducked around the examination table and came at Mervin from the side. His fist slid across Mervin's jaw, and the little man fell onto the floor with a scream. Bolan dove onto him and sought to twist the pistol out of his hand. As he grabbed it, a shadow fell across him, and Kraft's long arm caught him in the throat. Bolan flew backward into the examination table.

"Get up, Mervin," Kraft bellowed. "Get up, get out of here. *Vril-YA!*" He grabbed the front of Bolan's coat and hurled him against the wall. "The spear must be thrust, and Thylea ascendant!" Kraft vaulted onto the examination table and used it as a springboard, flinging himself at Bolan, who narrowly rolled aside. Bolan rose to his feet and barely avoided a looping backhand from Kraft, who was moving like a dervish, his bloody face contorted in a devil's mask.

They traded blows, punching and kicking, driving each other into walls and cabinets, as the base shook and shuddered about them. Somewhere close by, another set of pipes burst, and water began pouring down from the ceiling. Through the flurry of blows ringing down on him from his opponent, Bolan saw Mervin grab something from the counter closest to the examination table and then hurry for the hatch. The Executioner had a terrible premonition and tried to break away from Kraft, but the big man grabbed him in a headlock and spun him about, sending him slamming into the examination table, which toppled over, carrying the mummy in its plastic shroud with it.

As Bolan clambered to his feet, he saw Mervin standing in the hatchway, Bolan's own Desert Eagle in one trembling hand. Kraft backed toward him, eyes on Bolan. "Good, Mervin," he said. "We may not be able to complete your plan, but we have accomplished something."

"Oh, I'd say my plan is coming along just fine."

The Desert Eagle swung toward the big man. "Kraft," he said.

"Not now, Mervin. We must go. This place is coming apart at the seams."

"Yes, it is."

Bolan knew what was coming. Kraft must have heard something in his partner's voice, because he whirled even as the pistol roared. Kraft was knocked backward. Mervin fired at Bolan, who threw himself behind the examination table just in time. Then the little man stepped out of the hatch and slammed it shut.

Bolan reached the door a moment later. The mechanism had been jammed somehow, and no matter how much he forced it, it wouldn't budge. Water was slopping across the floor. It was now shin-deep, and the cold clawed at Bolan. He kicked at the hatch, cursing, but he wasn't strong enough to open it.

The sound of wheezing laughter made him turn. Kraft, sitting in the water, had pulled his wounded frame upright against the overturned table. He spat blood and shook his head. Bolan stared at him, impressed despite his loathing of the man. Kraft was tougher than most. "Cunning...little...sneak," he wheezed. "Braver than I gave him credit for... Never thought he'd shoot me like that."

Bolan looked down at Kraft. The Executioner knew a dying man when he saw one. The bullet hadn't killed him outright, but it had likely punched a hole in one of his lungs. A normal man would have been killed outright from shock alone, but Kraft wasn't planning on going that easily, it seemed. Bolan sank to his haunches. Kraft grinned redly at him. "You knew he was planning something?" Bolan asked.

"I knew he'd try something. He's…been difficult," Kraft grunted. He fumbled at his coat. Water splashed as HYPERBOREA made a sound like a dying beast. Bolan heard a distant bang that might have been an explosion or collapsing rocks. Kraft looked around blearily. "He wasn't a true believer. He lacked will."

"He's planning to sell the contagion," Bolan said. "I can stop him, if I can get that door open."

Kraft's gaze sharpened. He coughed again. His breathing was becoming more ragged. "You want me to help you," he croaked. "Why would I do that?"

"Because if you don't, people could die," Bolan said. "People *will* die." He realized as he said it that it was a mistake. Kraft was a psychopath, dedicated to a savage nihilism that would make even the most ferocious member of the Taliban balk. He wanted people to die—the more the better.

Kraft gave a caw of laughter that quickly descended into a strangled cough. "Good. Let them all die, the mud men and their filthy litters, let them all burn in the true fire." He grinned.

"They won't die alone. You said it yourself—Mervin isn't a true believer. He's betrayed you and your Society, all for a quick payday. He'll sell Ymir to the highest bidder—white, black or brown. Do you think he cares whether Aryans or Arabs buy it, so long as he gets paid? Do you want him to get away with that?" The words tasted ugly, and he spat them as fast as possible, puncturing the damp, cold air.

Kraft looked away. Bolan stared at him for a moment and then rose to his feet. "Then try and die quietly," the Executioner said. "I've got work to do."

Bolan went back to the door and tried to force it.

He heard the sound of Kraft climbing to his feet and then the dying man was beside Bolan, shoving his weight against the hatch's control mechanism. "*Vril-YA,* my friend," Kraft rasped. "What a warrior you would have made, had you but listened to the glory of your blood." The hatch gave a groan but didn't budge. Water from the burst pipes was thigh-high and didn't appear to be slowing down. Bolan cursed as his hands slipped on the wet metal. It tore his palms through his gloves and blood sluiced down the frame, mixing with the water.

"Keep pushing, my friend," Kraft whispered hoarsely. "Iron is nothing compared to will. Death is nothing." Bolan threw himself against the hatch, and Kraft did the same. The two men strained against the door, and then slowly, noisily, it began to open. The hinges, long since rusted, whined so sharply that Bolan's teeth itched in his gums. Bolan stumbled through the hatch and turned to see Kraft lying face-down in the water. The strain had done what the bullet alone couldn't. The Storm Eagle had made his last flight.

The Executioner turned away. There was no time, even if he had been inclined, to spare a thought for Kraft. The man had been a monster, but there had been steel to him.

The floor seemed to ripple beneath Bolan's feet. He had to hurry. There was no time for caution now, only for speed. Running flat out, the Executioner sought his prey.

HYPERBOREA was in its death throes when Bolan leaped from the entry hatch and slid onto the shaking gantry. He looked around and saw Mervin staring down at the rafts, as if calculating rate of descent and the statistical probabilities of surviving the fall. The water was churning below, stirred up by the creaking frame of the base. The whole structure was unraveling, like a house of cards struck by a strong breeze. Rocks were falling, as well, releasing trip-hammer-like sprays of mountain water that struck the base and hastened its collapse.

The gantry shifted, swinging slightly from side to side. Bolan maintained his balance through sheer will, and charged at Mervin. The little man noticed him at the last moment and turned, the Desert Eagle giving voice to his displeasure. The bullet skidded across Bolan's ribs and the wind was ripped from his lungs as he was forced to clutch the gantry rail for support. "Stop right there," Mervin yelled. "I'll shoot you again if I have to. I'm an excellent shot."

"I can't let you go," Bolan said, forcing himself to his feet.

"We can make a deal. Every man has his price," Mervin said. He reached into his pocket, found a squashed pack of cigarettes and pulled one out with his lips. He crumpled up the pack and tossed it away. "Except idiots like Kraft. That's why I shot him. He would have killed me! He would have happily condemned two-thirds of the human population to a very messy end, and for what? Some half-baked occult mutterings—some warrior! Ha! The look on his face when I shot him was itself almost worth the trip." He peered at Bolan over the barrel of the gun while he wrestled a lighter from another pocket. "How did you get out, anyway? I estimated that it would take you almost an hour to force the door."

"Kraft helped me," Bolan said.

"Kraft's dead." Mervin twitched nervously as the gantry writhed. He lit his cigarette and puffed madly.

"He is now."

Mervin gave a feral smile. "Good. Good. We can make a deal. Whoever you work for—they can have Ymir, if they meet my very reasonable price. Enough money to make Saul Mervin vanish and I'll be a happy man. I'm not greedy. I'm not a fool. Everything is going according to plan, and we can get out of here. You can help me get to the raft—not another step!" he shrieked, firing at Bolan's feet. "Not until we have a deal."

"No deals," Bolan said, pulling himself along the rail. He was getting his wind back, but he was still too far away for it to do him much good.

Mervin bit through his cigarette and spat it out. "Fine, fine, I don't need you. I didn't need Kraft, and I don't need you." His finger tightened on the trigger and Bolan hurled himself forward. HYPERBOREA shuddered and a loose strut fell, crashing against the gantry and tearing part of it away in a rhapsody of abused metal.

Bolan crashed into Mervin. They tottered for a moment, on the edge of the gantry. Then, the metal was ripped from beneath them and they plummeted into the chill embrace of the water.

Bolan hit first, and he felt as if he'd been struck by a sledgehammer. His limbs went limp as he sank momentarily into the darkness. Something passed by him, a plastic bag, holding what looked like fragments of bone. Then, Mervin was there, spearing right at him through a cloud of bubbles. The little man struck Bolan with the useless weight of the pistol, drawing blood from his scalp. Bolan tried to fight back, but between the blow and the impact of hitting the water, he lacked his normal precision. He felt sluggish and torn up inside and out. He hadn't even had time to take a breath.

Mervin kicked away from him and reached for the bag. Everything was moving in slow motion. Above, the light was blotted out by falling debris. Slow-moving missiles of steel and stone pierced the veil of the water's surface and speared downward into the darkness all around them. Bolan latched on to Mervin's coat and hauled himself after the little man. The bag was sinking, taking its deadly cargo down into the dark. Mervin screamed silently and began to thrash. His sharp elbow caught Bolan right in the bullet wound and he bucked in agony. Mervin twisted beneath him, punching him again and again as Bolan held tight.

If he allowed Mervin to get free, if he allowed him to reach the bag, it would all have been for nothing. The men that Mervin and Kraft had tortured to find the base, all the people injured or killed in their mad quest, they would all be denied justice. The Executioner refused to let that happen. Despite the hooks of pain and cold that tugged at his heart and lungs and mind, Bolan moved in for the kill.

Mervin clawed at him as Bolan grabbed his throat in a viselike grip. He squeezed and Mervin's struggles grew more frantic. The Desert Eagle, still in the other man's grip, struck him on the side of the head again and again, but Bolan didn't let go. The Executioner was determined that his enemy wasn't going to leave those dark waters, even if he himself had to die in the process. Dark spots roiled and burst at the edges of Bolan's vision and his lungs burned, screaming for oxygen. Mervin's hands found Bolan's throat and the two of them spun in slow circles in the water, each seeking to end the other. The little man was strong, far stronger than Bolan had realized. It was funny, in its way. He'd thought Kraft was the bigger threat—as Kraft himself had assumed—but the Tick-Tock Man was as nasty as any fanatic and twice as determined.

Bolan stared into Mervin's bulging eyes. In Kraft's eyes he'd seen madness and a vile dedication as well as fierce bloodlust, but in this man's stare he saw nothing save a darkness, an emptiness as vast as that which steadily called to them from below.

Then he felt a crunch as Mervin's trachea and neck bone gave way and the Tick-Tock Man went limp in Bolan's grip. His empty eyes did not fill or go blank; instead, they became as polished stones, opaque at last. Bolan released the body and shot for the surface without a second look, his muscles burning with cold fire as he clawed for the rising sun.

He surfaced with a gasp. Sucking cold air into his agonized lungs, he splashed toward the distant shore, knowing even as he made the effort that it wouldn't be enough. HYPERBOREA was collapsing around him, and the water was churning and dragging his exhausted body down. If the water didn't get him, a falling chunk of rock or metal would.

The Executioner refused to surrender. Doggedly, he swam. Then the sound of a motor filled his ears and he saw a raft speeding in his direction. A strong hand grabbed his coat, and Bolan forced himself to help his rescuer haul him into the raft.

"So, still think it was a good idea not to bring me?" Blackjack asked, looking down at him as she gunned the raft away from the base.

"I'm reevaluating my previous decision." Bolan coughed, spitting out water.

"Hey, so you didn't happen to find the keys to my plane, did you?" Blackjack said a moment later. "I just thought I'd ask, seeing as you sort of owe me."

Bolan didn't answer. Instead, he watched as HYPERBOREA sank like the lost continent it was named after and took its deadly secret into the depths. For the Executioner, that wasn't enough.

Not by a long shot.

22

Vienna, Austria

Four days later, the Executioner stepped off the U-Bahn tram into the Ringstrasse. Ferguson was waiting for him at the tram stop. He dropped his cigarette and stepped on it as Bolan threaded through the evening crowd toward him. Bolan wasn't surprised to see the FBI agent, though the man who was with him elicited a quirked eyebrow from the Executioner.

"Agent Chantecoq," he said mildly, as the French Interpol agent nodded in greeting. "How's Agent Tanzir?" Bolan had first run into Chantecoq and his subordinate Tanzir during a terrorist attempt to enter the States through Mexico.

"Quite well, Cooper. I shall inform her that you asked after her," Chantecoq said. "How are you finding Vienna?"

"It's lovely, in spots." Bolan looked at Ferguson. "I'm surprised you came yourself, Ferguson. It doesn't seem like your style."

Ferguson grimaced. "It's not. But sometimes you've got to do what you've got to do. Ogilvy was one of mine, and these bastards ordered his death. The Bureau takes care of its own."

"As does Interpol," Chantecoq said, lighting a thin cigarillo and expelling smoke from his nostrils. "These men have done awful things, Cooper. Not just in your United States, but in Europe, as well."

Bolan nodded. The three men were an oasis of stillness amidst the chattering crowd. It had taken him a day to recover from the ordeal he'd endured in Noatak, but when he'd woken from a solid twelve hours of sleep, he'd immediately made plans to hunt down the inner circle of the Society. The Tick-Tock Man and the Storm Eagle had been pawns, serving unseen masters. And it was those masters that the Executioner had come to Vienna to deal with.

Though HYPERBOREA was gone, and Ymir with it, there was no guarantee they wouldn't try again. If not Ymir, it would be something else. Fanatics, by definition, weren't easy to dissuade. Only death would stop them. Brognola had argued against his going alone, but the Executioner had insisted. He'd begun the fight alone, and he'd finish it the same way.

Sparrow had squawked loudly when he'd found out that his fellows were dead. He'd spilled everything he knew about the Society of Thylea, which wasn't much, in return for Bolan promising not to simply shoot him out of hand. A thorough search of various warehouses and residences owned by persons who did not strictly exist—despite owning property and credit cards—had given him a trail to follow. Kurtzman had been able to fill in the gaps with assistance from the CIA and Interpol.

The head of the FBI's Las Vegas office had traded

in favors with the CIA to gather the information the Executioner needed, with a bit of a push from Brognola. The Agency didn't like giving up the goods if they thought it'd be of use later, but Brognola had convinced them that it was past time for the Society of Thylea to become nothing but a bad memory. The Executioner could only guess as to Interpol's involvement, but he knew they likely wanted the Society out of the game as badly as the U.S. did.

"They're leaving today," Ferguson said. "Tonight, actually."

Bolan nodded. He'd known that already. The Executioner had spent the past thirty-six hours prowling Vienna, hunting down any lead he could find on the Society. He'd used the Beretta 93R that was currently holstered under his shirt more than once. The Society was readying itself to bug out, and they were sweeping any evidence of their existence under the rug. Bolan had traded shots with several of the group's soldiers in a hotel in the Innere Stadt and had put at least one in the morgue. Interpol had scooped the others up, by way of the police. Those agencies, in turn, had added to what he already knew. The Society was pulling up its wheels and preparing to go underground for a while, and Bolan intended to see that it was permanent.

"They're leaving from a private airfield near Vienna International Airport in Schwechat. The airfield's quiet—they've owned it since the Second World War—so you shouldn't have to worry about collateral damage." Ferguson handed Bolan a padded envelope. "There are directions in here and some other goodies," he said. "Photos and such."

"Where are they going?" Bolan asked.

"Who knows?" Ferguson said with a shrug. "They expended a lot of blood and treasure in this scheme of theirs and from what we can tell they're pulling out to regroup somewhere quiet. They own a few properties scattered about the continent—there's a castle in the Balkans, a villa on the Riviera and a few other spots. I figured you weren't planning on letting them get into the air. Or if you were…"

Chantecoq picked up the thread. "That you were planning on blowing them out of it, *oui?*" He made a fluttering gesture for emphasis, and Ferguson frowned. Bolan smiled grimly.

"Something close to that," he said.

"You don't have long. Once they're in the air, that's it. They'll scatter, and given the median age, most of them will be dead before we could bring any evidence against them," Ferguson said. "These guys are ancient."

"Old snakes still have fangs," Bolan said.

"Which is why theirs must be pulled, and quickly. They are reeling. Now is the time to put paid to several decades' worth of ghosts," Chantecoq said. He held out his hand to Bolan. "*Bonne chance,* Cooper."

Bolan shook his hand and nodded. He looked at Ferguson. The FBI man held out his hand, as well. As they shook, Bolan said, "What about Ackroyd?"

"Who's Ackroyd?" Ferguson said, turning away. "I don't think I know anyone by that name." Bolan watched them go until he'd lost sight of them in the crowd, and then he made his way quickly to the nearest S-Bahn stop. There was no sense in waiting.

On the ride out, Bolan thought about what had occurred after Blackjack had pulled him from the water. The pilot hadn't gotten her keys back, but she'd been happy enough with the reward she'd gotten for "assisting a law-enforcement agent in the course of his duties." It had been enough for a new hangar, at least. The Feds had taken over as soon as they'd arrived, arranging for the unfortunate campers to be debriefed and sign nondisclosure forms. From what he'd overheard, they were planning to make sure that no trace of the base or the manmade lake it had sat in was left. Explosives had been mentioned and significant geological renovation. They were following Ackroyd's suggestion, albeit several decades too late.

All that was left were the men who'd set everything into motion. He pulled the photos and directions out of the envelope Ferguson had given him. The men were all of a type. These were the sorts of men who employed people like Kraft and Mervin so they could keep their hands clean. They didn't look like men who wanted to burn down the world and stir the ashes, but Bolan knew that looks could be deceiving when it came to madness.

When he arrived, the private airfield was deserted, save for a single plane on the small section of tarmac. It was obviously awaiting the arrival of its passengers. The lights and noise from the nearby international airport lit up the night, but the airfield was quiet. Bolan pulled on a pair of gloves and vaulted the security fence. He stalked through the empty field toward the tarmac, the Beretta in his hand. He wasn't worried about security. They weren't expecting any trouble. The Sun-Koh—the inner circle of the Society of Thylea—were so insulated from the workings of

their servants that they had grown careless and arro-
gant. In many ways, they reminded him of the Mafia,
who'd become so used to being invulnerable they'd
forgotten what fear was. The Executioner intended
to remind them.

There were two men on guard, besides the pilot.
Both stood away from the plane, one near the boarding stairs and the other making a slow circuit of the
tarmac, his eyes sweeping the area. Bolan shot him
first, striding out of the darkness and putting a round
from the silenced Beretta directly between his eyes.
He was approaching the plane even as the guard fell,
the Beretta bucking once, twice, three times, as the
second guard stared at him in shock.

He fell, and Bolan stepped over him, boarding the
plane. The pilot was leaving the control cabin as Bolan
got on, and he froze as the Beretta twitched in his direction. *"Guten abend,"* Bolan said quietly. *"Spre-
chen sie Englisch?"*

"J-ja, ah, y-yes," the pilot said.

"Good. Please step outside the plane."

The pilot did as Bolan asked, hands held over his
head. Bolan had no way of knowing whether the man
was a member of the Society or just hired help. "You
have one chance at making it through tonight," he
said as they made their way down the stairs. "If you
do exactly what I say, you won't get what they got,"
he continued, indicating the dead guards.

"What do you want me to do?" the pilot asked.

"First, drag those bodies off the tarmac and into
the grass," Bolan said. He plucked the pistols from
the shoulder holster each man wore as the pilot did
so, keeping one and disassembling the other and toss-

ing the pieces out into the grass. When the bodies had been disposed of, Bolan pointed to the fuel drums that lined the wall of the nearby hangar. "Grab one of those and roll it over here," he said.

The pilot hastened to obey, and under Bolan's watchful eye, he rolled three drums out around the plane and opened them, allowing the fuel to splash across the tarmac. Bolan gave one a kick, causing it to vomit fuel in a wide circle. When the immediate area around the plane had been saturated, Bolan and the pilot rolled the drums back to their previous position and set them upright.

Then Bolan gestured toward the way he'd come. "Go," he said to the sweating pilot. The man looked at him as if he'd sprouted a second head. Bolan gestured with the pistol. "Go, and thank your lucky stars that I'm not like your bosses. Otherwise, I'd plant you out there with your buddies. Get out of here."

The man took off running. Bolan waited, watching him vanish into the darkness. There was a chance, though slight, he might try and warn his employers. But Bolan doubted it would occur to the pilot until far too late.

Bolan knew the Sun-Koh would be arriving in two cars. There were five of them, with at least a few guards.

He heard the growl of engines as he trotted across the tarmac and into the grass to wait. The plan was crude, but appropriate, he thought. It would have been too difficult to get explosives, and Interpol would have been reluctant to provide any more help than they already had. That meant he had to improvise. Luckily, he'd had a lot of practice.

The cars arrived right on schedule, pulling through the fuel and parking near the plane. The guards got out to open the doors for their employers. Bolan stood and took aim. The Beretta gave a loud hiss and the closest guard spun away, trailing red. The second clawed for his weapon, trapped beneath a buttoned coat. He never reached it. Bolan, much as he had earlier, stepped forward and fired, sending the man sliding across the hood of his car.

Bolan would mete out justice to these withered old men. It wouldn't be the kind of death they deserved, but Bolan wasn't a vengeful man. He fired a round at the tarmac, the bullet striking at just the right angle to elicit a spark. Flames reared up and began to crawl across the ground, heading for the vehicles.

The soldier waited patiently, ready to pick off the Society leadership as they emerged from the vehicle, seeking a place of safety. They had deserved worse, he knew. The deaths of those evil old men wouldn't erase the damage they had caused, or return the lives that had been lost because of their mad machinations, but no more innocents would suffer because of them.

For the Executioner, that would have to be enough.

* * * * *

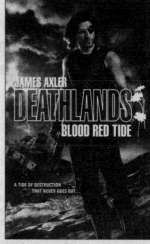

TAKE 'EM FREE
2 action-packed novels plus a mystery bonus

NO RISK
NO OBLIGATION TO BUY